CW01656510

The Last Castrato

J. Wolf Sanchez

Copyright © 2006 J. Wolf Sanchez

All rights reserved.

ISBN: 0-615-13045-3
ISBN-13: 978-0-615-13045-3
Suchamedia

ACKNOWLEDGMENTS

To the men and women who live and breathe their art, and sometime must suffer for it.

Prologo

Standing only a few feet away, I saw the man called Titino take a knife from his satchel. The naked body of my nine year old brother laid spread eagle on top of the upturned cart. My poor twin brother whom I loved deeply was unconscious now, while I was still awake and would soon bear witness to this unpardonable crime.

"Well? What are you waiting for?" Bragantti barked at Titino, who seemed to be in a daze.

Bragantti was the one who brought us here. He was a very big man. He was bald and his face had a meanness to it. He wore a perpetual scowl. Today was the first time I saw him smile. While my brother begged for mercy as he placed his massive hands on his tiny neck to asphyxiate him, I saw him smile.

Titino knelt on the dirt, his face inches from my brother's genitals. He gently cupped the scrotal sac and began to slice at the skin. Bragantti hovered over him, seemingly fascinated with the procedure. I thought I saw blood. I had to shut my eyes finally. As Bragantti said earlier, I was next.

Chapter 1

It was an hour before sunset, and the city of Florence was bathed in a golden light. There were only a few people on the street of the Via San Gallo that cool October day in 1877.

The old gas lighter had just begun his rounds, lighting each and every gas lamp that peppered the sidewalks. In 1875, Florence had acquired the gas lamps in its quest to keep up with the modern world, much to the apprehension of many Florentines who argued that their city would certainly go up in flames. A few even petitioned that the lamps be taken out. However, within a few months of the lamps introduction, their trepidation was slowly replaced by delight. Crime had gone down, shoppers and workers were able to stay out longer. In fact, if the lamps sole function was only to keep citizens from falling into a ditch in the dark, then that was already an advantage to itself! So the Florentines forgot all about their misgivings, and the gas lamps stayed.

Giuseppe was the Via San Gallo's gas lighter. He was a familiar face to many in this street. He was a happy man, they assumed, for he went about taking care of the lamps with diligence and efficiency.

On that chilly October afternoon, Giuseppe worked just as conscientiously. The darkness would soon engulf the whole neighborhood, and if he did not light the lamps at the end of the street by then, someone would surely complain. That complaint would be passed on to a councilman, who in turn would pass it to the director of public works. Unhappily, it would land on his supervisor's desk. His supervisor was a man a few years his junior. It was bad enough to be chastised by one so much younger. The worst part was that this very supervisor possessed an incredible ability to reprimand his subordinates in general public with verbal abuse the likes of which never been seen or heard by the community.

Despite the chill, Giuseppe stopped to wipe his brow with a dirty rag. He was getting far too old, he thought to himself. It was then he heard it. It was not the wind. It was someone singing. It was far too faint, much too unearthly. The hairs on the back of his nape rose. He turned around and noticed the large brass plaque on the wall of the building. It read *"L'ospedale di Bonifazio"*. He realized that he was standing directly across the main entrance of the imposing hospital. Giuseppe made a sign of the cross and jumped when the large doors burst open. He hurriedly walked away, not looking back. He lit all the lamps on that side of the Via San Gallo. He did not stop and rest until he got to the end of the street. *Santissima!* He cursed himself for being far too superstitious.

For many of the residents of the city of Florence in 1877, the happenings at L'ospedale di Bonifazio were shrouded in mystery and ambiguity, often fodder for gossip and speculation. The public of the time was fascinated by all things bizarre and unusual, which made the facility the perfect subject. L'ospedale di Bonifazio was not only a hospital for the physically ill. It was also an asylum for the insane.

Chapter 2

By the late 1800's, L'ospedale di Bonifazio was a Mecca for young men pursuing studies in the budding field of psychiatry. One such man was Randolph Bennett, a recent graduate who had just finished his residency and had chosen psychiatry as his branch of specialization.

His father, who was well to do, presented him with a gift. The senior Mr. Bennett asserted to his son the importance of travel as a means of furthering one's education. Any real gentleman of the time had at one point or another already visited a major capital or two. The world was waiting for such young men; Randolph would not be an exception. So Randolph found himself on a ship bound for Italy in the fall of 1877.

The voyage was neither ordinary nor remarkable. He was not seasick, except on the last night when some of the crew introduced him to grappa. After disembarking, he found an inexpensive hostel. Since Randolph had a few days to spare, he visited the usual tourist attractions, but nothing excited him as much as seeing a 'foreign' facility. He heard of the famous 'Bedlam' hospital in London, which would be the next stop on his travel itinerary. His colleagues had assured him though; Bonifazio was far more superior.

Prior to his leaving, his mentor Dr. Stanford had written one Dr. Uberto, the chief psychiatrist of Bonifazio about Randolph's wish to visit the hospital. The doctor wrote back saying physicians were always welcome to tour Bonifazio.

Contrary to some foreigners' impression, it was not named after the famous Saint Boniface they erroneously assumed it to be. The hospital was founded in the year of our Lord 1377 by Bonifazio di M. Ugolotti Lupi, then Marquis of Soragna.

Sometime between 1780 and 1785, the Grand Duke Peter Leopold, in keeping with his policy to improve the hygiene and health of the city of Florence, designated the hospital to admit all "incurables" (at the time, this meant that all those suffering from chronic illnesses such as infectious diseases and mental illness).

By 1788, the large hospital of Bonifazio officially began admitting psychiatric patients. So far, many of the city's chronically mentally ill were wandering the streets. The lucky few who had family to look after them were still at best treated harshly. Family members were at their wits end as to what to do with them, short of tying them down or locking them in their rooms. So the incurables soon found themselves guests of *l'ospedale.* They had long been a source of shame and inconvenience for the Florentines. Now, there was a place to put them.

Although it was some form of housing, a better definition would be that of incarceration. There was really not much treatment to begin with. The general public still regarded mental illness to be within the realm of the mystical or spiritual. However, in the early 18oo's, mental health care progressed with many experimental procedures and novel ideas.

After seeing the sights of Florence, Randolph Bennett found himself entering the intimidating edifice on Via San Gallo on that cold October day. The one thing that Randolph noticed immediately was that everything at Bonifazio was dark. It wasn't a lack of light, for there were ample sources of it. It wasn't the color scheme either. The walls were painted in what could be called 'institutional beige'. Instead, the darkness was felt. It was a heaviness that permeated its corridors and rooms. From the 14th century until that day, the constant stream of desperation had irrevocably left an almost psychic stain.

He came to a grand foyer and approached the counter situated in the center of the lobby. The monstrous and ornate desk carved from old mahogany seemed out of place. An older matron sat straight behind this construction, looking all grave and serious. He smiled at her and using his best Italian asked if she knew where was the office of Dottore Uberto was. She studied him carefully, peering from her glasses, unsmiling. She then answered him in rapid Italian. He could only smile and say *"Non ho parlato Italiano."* She asked, this time in stilted English, who he was. When he introduced himself as a doctor, visiting from America, she gave him a strained smile, much like a wolf in a hen house. She gave him directions in heavily accented, very broken English, gesticulating wildly. He nodded several times, trying very much to memorize her hand movements. It was then that she stopped.

"Ah, Dottore Uberto! Dottore Bennett from the America, he is looking for you!" Randolph turned around, and noticed the person the receptionist was addressing. Doctor Emilio Uberto smiled widely, displaying a gap between his two front teeth.

He was a large man, much larger and stockier than the average Italian man. If you took away the elegant suit and substituted a costume, Doctor Uberto could have been a strongman in any traveling circus.

He advanced toward Bennett, extending his rather

immense hands. Bennett thanked him for seeing him on such short notice. They spoke mostly about general matters. Bennett found out that Uberto's wife, who recently passed away, was also an American. They had been married twelve years, and she died giving birth. The baby did not make it either. It would have been a boy.

Dr. Uberto asked Randolph to join him in his office, so that he could catch up on newer treatments in America. The more they conversed, the more each discovered that they were very much alike, liking the same authors, fascinated by the same ideas. What was supposed to be an hour tour of the hospital stretched to a week, most of it spent discussing new theories regarding mental illness. They also spent a few good hours discussing music, since both were fans of *l'opera.* They dined out frequently. Being a bachelor again, Dr. Uberto spent many dinners alone. Bennett's company would be good for him.

Randolph spent the first few days at the hospital shadowing Dr. Uberto in his rounds at the lower floor, where the less chronic cases were. The doctor remained jovial and easy going. Dr. Uberto admitted that he saw in Randolph a young version of himself, full of passion with a fair amount of naiveté. One day, as they were discussing the genius of Bach, Dr. Uberto stopped and gave Randolph a wolfish grin.

"What?" Randolph asked. He couldn't help but smile, seeing his mentor's expression.

"How would you like to help me, Doctor Bennett?"

"I'd love to. What do you need help with, Dottore?"

"It would honor me if you would evaluate a long time resident of Bonifazio, as a courtesy."

"But of course, Doctor Uberto. I would be very glad."

Randolph was flattered at the invitation.

"You see, Randolph," the doctor said sadly, "I need new insight to a case that I find utterly fascinating and complex."

"Surely, you have more expertise, Dottore." Randolph said in a self-effacing tone.

"You do not understand. Let me explain this better. When you are too familiar with something, you may miss the little things, the details."

"And that's what you need me for, Doctor?"

"Precisely. I have not made any progress on this case. Maybe you will be luckier."

Dr. Uberto took a rather large folder from his drawer and slid it on the table between them. Randolph was flattered and thrilled at the same time. Trying his best not to seem outwardly too excited, he nonchalantly agreed. Over cups of espresso, the two then continued their conversation on music as Randolph stole glances at the chart before him, none of which was unnoticed by Uberto.

The clock struck four and Dr. Uberto managed to remember dinner with his late wife's family; today was her death anniversary. He begged Randolph's forgiveness and led the younger man out. Randolph agreed to meet the next day at eight in the morning in the hospital lobby, where Uberto could escort him and introduce him to the mysterious patient. Given the hurried manner of the older doctor, Randolph apologized that he too had a dinner engagement and said goodbye to his new friend. On his way to the lobby, Randolph realized that he forgot to pick up the chart. The chart that he had wanted so much to read before meeting the patient. It wouldn't do for him to run after Doctor Uberto. So he left also, quickly shaking off the silly thought that somehow, Uberto seemed too eager to leave, making him forget all about the records.

Chapter 3

The stench of the corridor was unpleasant, to say the least. Although the overworked staff of the hospital had tried their best to maintain a hygienic environment, vomit, urine and feces that the residents of the hall gladly provided had by now become part of the decor. No matter what kind of disinfectant the staff of Bonifazio had used could not overpower the odor which by now entrenched itself on the walls and floor. Randolph Bennett realized this as an aide unlocked the door that led to the ward that housed the incurables. He came to a vestibule where a couple of nurses in crisp, starched uniforms and a muscular aide congregated behind a counter. One of them was talking to Dr. Uberto, who was wearing a pristine white smock, the standard uniform of physicians at the time. Randolph Bennett thanked his lucky stars that he managed to bring his own. The older doctor spotted him. "Dottore Bennett!" Uberto advanced to crush Bennett in a most masculine embrace. After exchanging the usual pleasantries, Dr. Uberto led the way to the end of the malodorous corridor.

"You will be evaluating a certain Signor Giaochinno Vespucci, a long term resident of L'ospedale. He has a plethora of neurosis and mania." Uberto put his hands in his pockets, apparently searching for something, still walking.

They moved slowly down the long and narrow corridor, past busy and harried aides coming in and out of rooms. One resident, dressed in the standard hospital gown, made his way out in the hallway. Dr. Uberto said hello to him, addressing the patient by name. Uberto then led the poor man back to his room, just a few steps away.

"So this Signor Vespucci, Dottore? I take it he hasn't responded to any of the standard treatments?" Bennett asked cautiously.

"Signor Vespucci has not responded well," Uberto sighed.

"I'm afraid I haven't had the chance to read his chart yet, sir." Randolph remarked sheepishly, afraid that such a statement would warrant him a negative opinion for Dr. Uberto. Meanwhile, an aide approached them and whispered something in Dr. Uberto's ear. Uberto smiled and nodded a few times. The aide left.

"Perhaps this way is better." Uberto smiled wanly. "The chart, it does not give you the true psyche of the man. It will only tell you the facts." The two walked down the long corridor.

"Can you tell me some history then, Dottore?" Dr. Uberto stopped. He spoke as he searched his pockets again.

"Ah, si…Signor Vespucci was found clutching his fiancée's dead body. He was covered in her blood, holding the dagger that killed her. He claims it was his younger brother, his fraternal twin Vincenzo, who forced him to kill her. You see, he loved his brother very much."

"This was the precipitating factor for his mania then." Randolph interjected. "Whatever happened to his brother?"

Uberto finally found what he was looking for and fished out a large ring of keys from his left hip pocket.

"Perhaps you should ask Signor Vespucci. He can tell you the story much better than I.

"Can he?"

"He has moments of lucidity, although they are

infrequent. Do not worry. Signor Vespucci is a true polyglot. He speaks French, English and German aside from his native Italian. He was- is-- a most remarkable man. Many say he's a genius."

Dr. Uberto gave Randolph a paternal glance and continued. "Anyway, I have not been able to get him to share with me his thoughts. You might be luckier than I."

Uberto went through the keys on the ring and chose a rather larger, older looking one. "He will make a fascinating case study for you. You are an avid musicologist. We've discussed if music could heal that broken mind. He will be a perfect case for you then."

"Yes, you said that earlier, Doctor Uberto."

"Dottore Bennett, what I didn't mention is that Signor Vespucci is *L'ultimo*... the last of them..."

"The last-- what?"

They stopped at a large, oak door.

"The Last Castrato." Uberto sighed deeply.

"Castrato!" Bennett exclaimed. Uberto seemed pleased at his surprise.

"Signor Vespucci started out as a choir boy," Uberto said, "him and his brother both. Their father, a drunk and good for nothing, sold them."

"Sold them? Isn't that illegal?"

"No, no..." Uberto chuckled. "Not sold like slaves. It was common back in the time to 'sell' children to a patron of the arts and music. The patron would pay the family for the opportunity to sponsor these gifted boys. Signor Vespucci and his fraternal twin were nine or ten years old at the time, nearing puberty. Their angelic voices needed to be preserved." Uberto singled out a key and inserted it into the keyhole.

"Castration..." Bennett winced.

"Si, their father permitted it, in the hope that the fame, as well as the fortune that came with being a great castrato would come to them. They were very poor."

"But that's barbaric!" Randolph heard his voice echo down the corridor.

"Si, barbaric," Doctor Uberto agreed.

"I mean, what did they use for anesthetic?"

"Sometimes opium, but other times, bilateral pressure on the carotid vessels."

"They were strangled?" Bennett asked in disbelief.

"Only to the point of unconsciousness," Uberto explained.

Bennett saw the logic and added, "So they wouldn't feel the pain." Uberto nodded.

"Si. According to hearsay, there was not sufficient pressure applied to Vespucci. He woke up as they were severing the spermatic cords. Before passing out again, he saw his brother, lying across from him. His brother had already gone through the same process first."

"Oh, my God." Randolph muttered under his breath.

"Yes, our Signor Vespucci is probably the last of his kind. The world has no need of the castrato anymore." Uberto inserted the key again. The massive door creaked open ominously.

"I will leave you two alone. If there is anything you need, just call out. I will have an aide placed just outside this door momentarily." Uberto closed the door behind him. Bennett heard the unmistakable click of the lock.

Bennett found himself standing in a tiny room, possibly eight or nine foot square, much like a monk's cell. A small window placed high afforded only enough light for Bennett to make out his surroundings. A wooden pallet was to his right, with a dirty mattress on top of it. Beside it was a small bucket. In the farthest corner of the room, a man in a straitjacket, on his haunches. The man was rocking himself, humming an unknown melody.

"Signor Vespucci, my name is Doctor Bennett." Bennett was taken aback by how loud his voice sounded. Much like a dagger placed against the flesh, he felt the sharpness of his voice

"Bennett..." The old man repeated flatly, without looking up.

"I need to ask you a few questions..."

The old man's face lit up. "Do you know Vincenzo?"

"No. I'm afraid not. Signor Vespucci, how old are you?"

The man stood up and laughed. His laughter had a melodic quality to it. Much like a boy's laugh. It was neither feminine nor masculine. With the window above him, Vespucci's face was hidden in the shadows.

"Do you like music, Dottore?"

"Yes," Bennett answered. "Yes I do."

"Do you love music so much that you see it, you breathe it, you need it to remain alive?"

"Well, I think our lives would not be complete if..."

"Yes!" Vespucci hissed.

Bennett felt that his answer was sufficient to establish good rapport with the patient. Rapport was the necessary ingredient towards getting the patient to open up.

"It begins with rhythm..." Vespucci said low. "Listen. Everywhere there is rhythm. Even our heart beat is rhythm." Bennett felt that he was being lectured. "Signor Vespucci...."

The frail, old man began to hum.

"Signor Vespucci. I know that music was an important part of your life. It is mine. Perhaps we can talk about music then."

Vespucci stopped humming and stepped out of the shadows. He came closer, too close.

As a physician, Bennett always allowed a certain space between himself and his patient, most especially when the patient had the tendency to become physically aggressive. However, Vespucci was restrained, Bennett reasoned. It would be difficult if not impossible for him to get out of that strait-jacket. Vespucci's mouth was now a few inches from his ear. Then, he said "Music is life." said the old man, whispering in an almost conspiratorial manner. Vespucci then backed away quickly. He looked at the floor and began to mutter something in Italian.

"Maybe you could tell me the first memories you have of music?" Bennett suggested.

"Do you know Bach's *Misa*?"

"But of course, yes."

"Ah," the answer pleased the old man. "Dottore Uberto does not. He is an opera man. Much like the man who claims to love reading, but only limits himself to novels." Bennett remained silent, to keep the man talking.

"The music of my life is not an opera. It is a mass--" he said very low.

Bennett knew the patient was testing him.

"I may tell you a story," Vespucci continued.

"Do you want to hear the story?

Bennett said yes.

"Then you need a key."

A key? Was Vespucci asking for the keys to the door?

No, that would be too obvious.

"To open, you need a key."

The answer came to Bennett. It was obvious. He knew the famous Mass by Bach. Bennett inhaled then said *"Kyrie Eleison, in B minor."*

Vespucci looked up at him for the very first time. Bennett still had to strain however to see all of the man's features, still hidden partially in the dark.

"Va bene, va bene." There was contentment in his voice. Vespucci began to walk towards him, shuffling in a way that most very old men do. The light from the window fell on him, finally revealing his face.

"Once upon a time, years and years ago, in the year of our Lord eighteen hundred and five, there was a beautiful woman named Gabriella..."

Randolph noticed that the old man's face was wrinkled, his skin mottled and gray. His hair was gray and very long, almost to his shoulders. It was beginning to thin. But what surprised Bennett were the old man's eyes. They were the deepest blue he had ever seen. Blue as the sky.

Chapter 4

About thirty five miles south of Florence lies the small city of San Gimignano. From afar, it looks picturesque, almost dream-like. Approached closer, one begins to notice the structures jutting out insolently from the town's center, defying the landscape. These are San Gimignano's towers. The wealthy families that controlled the city back in the Middle Ages built some 72 tower-houses as symbols of their affluence and power. Each family, trying to outdo the other, built towers that sometimes would reach as high as a hundred feet. Of the seventy two towers built, only fourteen remained. The fourteen miraculously preserved towers each reflected a period of confrontational one-upmanship in Italian history. San Gimignano was perched on a hill, and its towers seemingly looked like they were reaching for the heavens.

By 1813, visitors who arrived at San Gimignano were confronted with buildings in all manners of styles. As if some attention deficit architect was given free rein, each house and church stood vying for architectural attention. Some buildings reflected the Romanesque, while others the Gothic. Around the corner, there was a church in the neoclassical style.

However, these same visitors did not make the trek to San Gimignano to come look at the crumbling towers or the dissimilar structural designs. Almost all of them were lovers of music, and they came to hear the boys' choir that performed in the cathedral of San Gimignano.

In a country where music and the visual arts abound, every artist had to make the effort to stand out and be noticed. What made this particular choir stand apart from the rest was they made it seem effortless. Their voices, many claimed, were short of angelic. Recently, the Archbishop of Milan was heard to exclaim that although Milan could boast of the finest choirs and musicians, it lacked a boys' choir that could hold a candle to San Gimignano's. Word of mouth spread about the pure perfection of the *'ripieno'* of Bach's Saint Matthew's Passion. Many who heard the boys told their friends and family, using terms such as 'enchanted', 'magical' and 'guileless.' The boys' choir sang regularly at the Cathedral.

This cathedral, was dedicated to St. Mary in 1575. It was not very large, if one went by the European standards of how large a cathedral should be. Nor was it extraordinarily beautiful outside. But what it lacked outside was easily augmented by the music that swelled from within. On any given special occasion, one could hear the choir singing.

For several years there was no choir and there was no music. There was an organ, but the organist who regularly played it had long since died, and the instrument was silent. Its silence became an invitation to rodents who took up residence, maliciously taking a nibble here and there of its components. However, all that changed three years ago, when a sad looking priest arrived carrying only a banged up suitcase and a cello.

The sad looking priest was Father Nicolo Battista Russo. He was an average built man with a shock of gray hair on his handsome head. He had just turned fifty-three. He entered the seminary at what some considered a very late age of twenty-two. He was a gifted musician. When he was twenty, he was awarded second prize for his composition. It was even performed at the Milan Festival of the Arts. Nicolo could have made a decent living as a musician, but could not ignore what he claimed to be his true vocation. Finally, after much fasting and prayer, he decided to enter the seminary. He graduated and was ordained. Because of his extraordinary musical skills, he was put to work, spending most of his priesthood in charge of the music of the church. He spent nearly three decades of his life in Milan. He ended being the director for music for the diocese of Milan, where he assisted the Archbishop in all matters of ceremony.

Father Russo was happy in Milan, feeling very much fulfilled in his parochial duties. On some occasion, the Archbishop would need him to play his instrument as after dinner entertainment, when the elegant ladies and gentlemen would sit to listen to music, so as to help aid in the digestion. One such night, he brought his cello and played exceptionally well. So well in fact that one certain woman had paid special attention to him the whole evening after his performance.

The Lady Renata Mulieri, third cousin to the Duke of Calabria, was a very vindictive woman. She had recently found out that her husband was unfaithful. Perhaps it was Father Russo's talent that made him appealing to her. Or maybe the thought of him being a priest became a subconscious challenge. Whatever her reasons, she took an immediate liking to Nicolo Russo. She also wanted to get back at her husband.

She invited him many times for dinner, on the premise of putting on a concert that would benefit the cathedral and the church itself. At first, Nicolo, naïve in the ways of women, honestly thought that his musicianship was needed. The Lady Renata began to drop hints, but still it went over his head. Finally, her ladyship could no longer contain herself and in a moment of weakness, threw herself on him, swearing eternal love. She covered him with kisses, much to the complete shock of Nicolo! Father Russo, following a strict code of celibacy scorned the lady's advances. Distressed and highly alarmed, he had no choice but to run way. He found himself half an hour later blubbering like an idiot before the Archbishop in his study. The Archbishop listened and told him to keep the embarrassing episode to himself till he had a chance to figure out what to do next. When the Archbishop woke the next morning, he was not surprised to find the lady's maid with a message for him, requesting him for an audience. He wrote her back, granting her request, arranging an early afternoon meeting.

The lady arrived with none other but her famous cousin, the Duke of Calabria. Outraged by Nicolo's rejection, her ladyship used all her feminine powers to make sure that he was punished, no, excommunicated! She then proceeded to howl and wail about the near molestation of her person upon the hands of one Father Nicolo Russo. She proceeded to go over how she and Father Russo would meet, how the priest would drop suggestions, hinting at the possibility of a tryst. She understood perfectly well that the attention she had paid to Father Russo was misinterpreted. Maybe her beauty was too much for him? Whatever it was, there was simply no justification.

The Archbishop, proficient in matters diplomatic comforted the Lady and assured her that he would see to the matter, without really having promised anything. He guaranteed the Duke that it would be resolved in the best possible way. He could not call the lady a liar, most especially in front of her esteemed cousin!

When her ladyship and the Duke left, (seemingly satisfied) the Archbishop grieved. He had grown very fond of Father Russo. Knowing Father Russo's moral fortitude and principles, he did not believe a single word of the accusation. Still, it would not do to cross the Duke. Father Russo would have to be relocated. After conferring with his confessor, the Archbishop called Father Russo to his office. He explained that he was being transferred to San Gimignano because of the recent occurrence. The priest begged forgiveness, if there was anything to forgive, and beseeched the Archbishop not to send him away. He got on his knees and sobbed, clutching the hem of the Archbishop sultana. But the Archbishop had no choice.

Upon his arrival at San Gimignano in the spring of 1811, Father Russo, despondent over his exile, stayed mostly in his room. Of course, he still had to assume his ministerial duties, but there was no joy. He simply went through the priestly motions. He said mass, heard confession and married young couples. He baptized babies and buried the dead. He went through the gestures, but deep down, he despaired. He was lost in this church. He was lost because he felt he was being punished unjustly. Still, he tried to find it in his heart to forgive the Archbishop, her ladyship, the Duke, the carriage driver and even the horse that brought him here. Every day, before he went to bed, he asked that God grant him serenity to accept his lot. He retired to every night, praying for a sign that his deportation was God's will.

Father Russo's gloom was further aggravated by the fact that there was no more music. Whereas in Milan he had availability of the best musicians, here in San Gimignano, there was nothing. The organ in the cathedral had long fallen into disrepair, sounding like an accordion in the throes of persistent respiratory distress. There was no choir to speak of. No choir? Why should there be? For the last few years, no one competent enough was there to assist in the endeavor. The parish priest that he had replaced was a closet gambler, the one before that an alcoholic. Neither had the time nor inclination for anything musical.

A few weeks later, Monsignor Cosetti, his direct supervisor and confessor asked him if he had given any thought into starting a choir; a boys' choir. Russo assented, first out of sheer obedience. He wanted to say no, out of spite, but his humility overturned his pride.

He then realized that God did have a reason for him to be in San Gimignano. It was to bring music back to the silent church! He was mildly excited at this revelation. By the end of the week, he was downright ecstatic, conferring with Benedetto, the sacristan, about what pieces they could perform. He chose Benedetto for two reasons. Benedetto, the church's sexton, had arrived a few weeks before he did. They were both strangers in a strange land. Secondly, Benedetto was already in the employ of the church. Most importantly, he had a very good ear for music. He was an accomplished player of the viola.

They spent days talking about simple compositions that a fledging boys choir should tackle first. They wrote to Milan to send them some copies of music. They poured over a few choral pieces they found in the organist's loft and set about simplifying the arrangements. It was then that Father Russo began to feel very anxious. What if there were no boys wishing to join the choir? Or worse, what if those who did join sang terribly? He remembered one boys choir that he heard a while back perform a *requiem* mass. They brayed like mules, assaulting the dear father's ears! Silently, Father Russo prayed for a miracle. Later that week, during mass, the Monsignor announced that auditions would be held for a boys choir Friday morning. A sign was also put out announcing the on-coming auditions.

By Thursday night, Father Russo, who normally slept well, tossed in bed. He finally fell asleep as the roosters began their crowing. Sweating profusely, he woke up from a terrifying dream about a choir made up of a hundred boys, all looking like the Lady Renata herself. The boys, (or maybe the women, since they were dressed like women, but had the faces and bodies of children.) gave chase with pitchforks in hand. They cornered him, calling him all kinds of names. As they were about to stab him, Russo screamed. Thankfully, that was also when he woke up. He crossed himself, grateful that he was not stabbed. It was a superstition that if one was killed or died in his dream, his heart would stop and he would also die a physical death. He slowly struggled out of bed and got ready to say the early mass.

When the five o'clock mass was done, Father Russo walked to the nearby parsonage and had breakfast. Then he called for Benedetto. Together they walked back to the church. In the tiny alcove where the priests changed vestments, he spotted Francesco, the altar boy. Russo ordered him to follow them. The trio entered the sanctuary. Father Russo fought his growing anxiety, fearing that there wouldn't be any boys willing to try out.

He opened the door and was flabbergasted. Nearly one hundred and fifty boys from all over the small city had showed up. That was not counting the parents and a motley collection of relatives and well-wishers.

The boys in general were a quiet bunch. It was the parents, mostly mothers, who contributed to the cacophonous hum that reverberated throughout the church. Mothers telling their sons to sit still, to smile, to keep quiet. Hands flattened wayward hair, thumbs brushed cheeks of grime.

Father Russo immediately decided to stop this from turning into a nightmare. He looked at Benedetto and told him to be ready. The young sexton nodded, unsure of what Father Russo meant by 'ready.' Father Russo then walked and stood in front of the altar. In a most commanding voice he explained that it was now seven a.m. He would see all the boys at a specific time. The crowd began to quiet down, lest they missed a word.

Father Russo then said that the children, whose surnames began with 'A' through 'F' would be seen between now until ten a.m. Those whose surnames began with the letters 'G' through 'L' he would see between ten and noon. At noon, they would break for lunch and continue at one pm. 'M' through 'R' from one until three, and finally children whose last names began with 'S' to 'Z' would be seen from three till five. Meanwhile, everyone needed to leave. They could wait outside, or go home and come back. Benedetto took the cue and began to usher all the people out. The pushier parents tried to talk him into seeing their children first. Why, they had traveled farther than the rest or my boy is too frail to wait outside that long. Father Russo merely repeated almost word for word the protocol that he would follow. Finally, the sanctuary was cleared. The door was shut by the pimply altar boy, who was more than happy to assist Father Russo and Signor Benedetto in this endeavor. When Father Russo asked Francesco if he would try out for a part in the choir, the boy shook his head and laughed. He told the good father that he was stone cold, tone deaf.

So it began. Boy after boy was ushered in by Francesco, while their parents were told to wait outside. One couple tried to squeeze their way in. Father Russo told them that they could not watch, and told them that the audition would not progress until they vacated the premises. Then Father Russo called the faithful sexton over. He whispered something to Benedetto, who disappeared. The parents stood still, uncertain as to what to do next. Father Russo asked them again if they would leave. The mother claimed that the boy could sing better if she was around. The priest crossed his arms and gave her his sternest expression. She sighed, patted the boy on the head, kissed him twice on the cheek and dragged her frail looking husband out. All the while, the large woman muttered about how some people could be so dictatorial.

Benedetto then reappeared, armed with a large slate. He had written in chalk that any parent or relative escorting their offspring in would automatically disqualify the child. Benedetto asked Francesco to hang the slate outside the door, where a nail was already in place. Francesco was only happy to oblige, knowing this new directive would produce much more anxiety among the adults, whom he thought was an ambitious lot. A group came to read the message. They in turn told the others. Even though the adults didn't like it, they still respected the Father's dictates. They really had no choice.

The morning produced a handful of boys who sang exceptionally well. Benedetto took down their names and told them to come back next week. Most of them were told that they sang well enough, but weren't told anything else. Francesco would escort them outside and call the next boy in. Then, he would tell the parents of the last boy that Father Russo thanked them for coming, and that he could try again next year. A few didn't take the rejection well and tried to reason with Francesco, who merely smiled and said he was just the messenger.

By the end of the day, Father Russo had about 40 boys. Although all good singers, there was something missing. At about quarter to five, Francesco ushered in two boys.

"The Vespucci brothers, Father," Francesco announced.

"They are twins," the young man continued, as if that fact was not obvious enough. Francesco also added that the two boys were the last to be seen. The Zucco boy had left, feeling faint and nauseous.

Father Russo looked at the two. Not identical, although extremely close to be called that. They both looked to be about seven years of age, maybe younger. He really couldn't tell. He looked at Benedetto.

"Do we listen to them both or one at a time?" the old priest asked. Benedetto shrugged. Finally, Father Russo asked who was older.

"I am, sir." The one on the right replied. Slightly larger and taller than the one on the left. A very slight difference though, almost imperceptible at a quick glance.

"And what is your name?" the priest asked.

"My name is Giachinno Vespucci, sir" the young boy squeaked. "And this is my brother Vincenzo."

Vincenzo smiled shyly, in the manner most shy boys do. The priest tried very hard not to smile. These boys were disarming. But what did they sound like?

"Do you know any songs?" Father Russo asked.

"We know lots of songs!" Giaochinno offered. Realizing his familiar tone, he quickly corrected himself and said more solemnly, "Vincenzo and I know many songs, Father, sir."

It did not escape the priest that the boy corrected himself, and recognized the authority of the priesthood. That would be in their favor.

"All right," the father said, "Sing something then."

Giaochinno nodded slightly to Vincenzo, who smiled again. Then Giaochinno opened his mouth. As the sun filtered through the window of the cathedral, Father Russo heard a sound unlike any other and it filled the sanctuary. Giaochinno began the first verse of the *Ave Maria* by Giovanni Artusi. Extremely elegant, Giaochinno couldn't have chosen a more appropriate song. Then, in the middle of the song, Vincenzo began to sing too. The boy's voices were almost duplicates of each other. But the way Vincenzo sang counterpoint to the melody made it even more poignant, haunting and evocative. When the song ended, Father Russo realized that he had unknowingly shed tears. He turned to Benedetto who sat next to him, mouth opened like a bass out of water. Even the tone deaf Francesco had a look of wonder about him. God had brought Father Russo the answer to his prayers. In His infinite goodness and mercy, God not only sent one, but two miracles that day.

Chapter 5

The boys whom Father Russo had prayed for were also the product of much prayer on someone else's part. To know the whole story however of how they ended at Father Russo's church, one will have to go back a few years.

It was the summer of 1802, which proved to be a more bearable summer to the residents of San Gimignano than the previous year. The olive groves promised a good crop. Small industries were springing up, boosting the flagging economy of the sleepy town. Everyone was happy. Happier still was Lorenzo Vespucci, a twenty seven year old widower and plasterer. He had just proposed to Gabriella Assumpta, whom many considered to be the prettiest girl in the entire neighborhood. Lorenzo, who was affectionately called Enzo by everyone, had been married before, but it had been two years since his wife Secunda died in a boating accident. Secunda, silly girl that she was, went boating with her cousins even though she couldn't swim. When the boat capsized, everyone else swam for shore. Secunda however, did not make it to shore. She was found later that afternoon, face down in the water. Enzo didn't even miss her really. He neither loved nor cared for his first wife. He married her out of lust.

After Secunda's funeral, Enzo began to live the life of a bachelor again. He vowed he would never get married again, after experiencing the more distressing side of matrimony. Instead he drank more, worked less and pretty much did as little as he could.

One day, his mother told him to pick up some fish from the market. He complained, saying that it was a woman's job. She said if he wanted dinner that night and every other night he better do as he was asked. Grumbling, he asked for money. She gave him some, warned him about not spending it on 'other' things. What things? He asked. As far as he knew, Enzo had not bought anything for himself. *Stupido!* Enzo's mother rapped him upside the head. "Do you not hear the gossip? You work very little, and the little you make is spent on getting intoxicated!" Annunziata screeched. He didn't care.

"Let them talk," he whined. His mother merely stuffed the money in his hands and left away grumbling. Enzo left too. He was to help old man Grigio whitewash the outside of a house, and Grigio would share with Enzo what they paid him, which was not a lot but enough to get him some liquid libation.

Enzo, experienced plasterer that he was, did badly at whitewashing. At the end of the day, he was nearly covered in the putrid stuff. He and Grigio went their separate ways after dividing the money. He was on his way to the tavern when he remembered the fish. Damn the fish! Well, he would either get the fish or go hungry. Given the fact that he didn't have lunch that day, his stomach dictated his next move. The tavern could wait.

The market was busy, filled with mothers and wives doing last minute shopping. He approached the first stall that he saw and found out it was all produce. He kept looking. Finally he found a stall that sold fish. But what to get? He never did the marketing. He cleared his throat and said *scusi* to the lady who had her back turned to him. When she turned around, Enzo's heart skipped a beat. She was beautiful. Not beautiful in a way Secunda had been, but refreshing and innocent. Enzo, who had never fallen in love, fell hard. She took one look at him and then she laughed. She covered her mouth but her laughter was so delightful and infectious that Enzo started laughing too. He realized that this was the first time in two years that he laughed like this. He paused and asked her what was so funny. She said that he looked like a ghost. He realized that the whitewash still covered much of him. He laughed at the preposterous idea that she thought him a ghost. When their laughter had died, he asked for her name. She wouldn't tell him though. It was bad enough that the other sellers looked at her as she laughed like a loon. Enzo however, made sure he introduced himself. He bought his fish and tried to make small talk. Unfortunately, the young girl's mother arrived to tell her to pack up, it was already late. She complied readily, leaving Enzo holding his fish, still looking like a ghost.

That night, he couldn't stop thinking about her. The next morning, he asked his mother that since the fish was so good last night, could he have it again? Signora Vespucci, flattered that her son thought so highly of her cooking, regretfully told him there was no more left. Enzo replied that he wouldn't mind passing by the market again, to get more fish. As luck would have it, old man Grigio had another job for him. A real job, where his plastering skills were needed. So, he would see her after work again.

He did see her. She in turn was charmed by him. He bought fish every day for that week.

He then started to leave her letters of love and devotion, love in a language dripping with sweetness. Letters filled with words so syrupy that bees could have feasted on them. She would blush when he arrived to hand her these notes. The first time, she left the letter on the stall's counter, afraid to touch it. But that first one that she did not pick up right away got wet and barely legible. So she always made sure that she put it away as soon as he set it down. Not to mention that she was deathly afraid that someone else pick it up. Her mother, perhaps? *Madonna!* She would be beaten for sure.

During the next few weeks, Enzo began to look better. He started taking care of himself again. He begged his old boss to take him back (which he did) and forgot all about the tavern. One day, he asked if Gabriella (for that was her name) would let him walk her home. She refused. So he followed her. When he found out where she lived, he went the next day to surprise her. He had bathed, combed his long, black hair and put on his best clothes. When he got to her house, he spied Gabriella's mother trying desperately to carry a large bundle of firewood up the path. Seizing the opportunity, he rushed to her aid. She thanked him and immediately stated that his wife was a lucky woman. He replied that he was not married. He told her the sad story of Secunda's passing, cutting out the ugly parts. She then wondered if he would be so kind to look at the well behind the house, whose bucket was stuck and could not be dislodge by her weak arms. Again, he gallantly obliged. By the end of the morning, Gabriella's mother thought him a likely candidate for her daughter and invited him to dine that night with them, as a token of gratitude to him for all his hard work. He readily agreed.

When Gabriella arrived, her mother told her to freshen up, for she wanted her to be presentable. Gabriella groaned inwardly. She knew she would have to sit through another boring dinner, for her mother took matchmaking seriously. Unfortunately, the three men that she had invited to dinner in the past few months were all *inutile*, which in Italian could be best translated as useless. One was extremely old, ready to kick the bucket any time. The other was extremely stupid, made obvious by his extremely limited vocabulary. The last guest was so obnoxious that even Gabriella's mother was forced to end the dinner earlier than usual. But her mother assured her that this one was a keeper. She began to described how dashing this one was, how gallant. Gabriella didn't care. Her heart was set on Enzo, her little ghost.

That night, who else showed up for dinner but Enzo himself, who winked slyly and smiled smugly at her. She was scarcely able to contain herself that she had to excuse herself to check on the dinner cooking in the kitchen several times. There were a few more dinners after that. Two months later, he asked Gabriella's mother for her daughter's hand.

On September 9, 1804, Enzo and Gabriella were married. The wedding was extremely modest, far more humble than his last one. The bride wore a simple white dress, which belonged to her mother when she was married. It had to be hemmed again and taken in.

The reception was a simple affair, held at the small private garden behind the church. There was much laughter and singing. Enzo kept his new bride close, entertaining her with his observations about the wedding guests. His constant remarks kept Gabriella in a constant state of giddiness. It was a happy occasion for both of them. As the guests began to leave, Signora Vespucci hugged her new daughter-in-law tightly and gave her unsolicited advice: Make sure that the pasta wasn't too limp, the sauces not too tart, and that Enzo had a clean white shirt every Saturday when he joined the old men at their game of bacci.

Chapter 6

The month of June saw torrential rains pound the roofs of San Gimignano. Many of the residents stayed indoors, knowing that the rains were a blessing form heaven. The children however, were disgusted, having to stay inside and help with the chores. In the Vespucci household, Gabriella fretted that her pregnancy had advanced too far. The midwife had informed her that the baby was due on the first week of June. It was now June 15, 1805, but still no contractions. Another reason she fretted was that she was so big. The women folk that she had seen with child had never been this huge. She felt like a whale, and suffered from fits of depression. Enzo stayed home too. They had finished a job two days ahead of schedule, which pleased both his boss and their employers.

They had sat down for dinner. Enzo's mother joined them. She announced that she had consulted the neighborhood seer, who assured her that Gabriella would give birth to a girl. If that was the case, then she should be named after her, she suggested. Gabriella winced. Annunziata, her mother-in-law's name, was unpleasant to her ears.

Actually, this was not the first time that the older Signora Vespucci recommended this. The fact was she proposed it the very day that Gabriella found herself pregnant. Gabriella told her that she would think about it, but deep down, she had already settled on the name 'Catarina', which she thought to possess such an exotic ring to it. Enzo chuckled. His mother could be so stubborn.

Gabriella excused herself to fetch some water. Enzo told her he would get it, but Gabriella explained that walking around was good for her. While Enzo and his mother made small talk, Gabriella went to the kitchen. As she put down her mug on the counter, she felt something warm run down her legs. Enzo called to her, but there was no answer. Enzo went to the kitchen to find Gabriella still standing with a quizzical expression. Enzo looked at her then looked down. He became aware that by his wife's feet was a small puddle. *Madre mia!* The roof had sprung another leak, he thought. He silently cursed, knowing that this would be another expense. While he was looking up the ceiling, Signora Vespucci entered the kitchen wondering why she was abandoned at the dinner table. Gabriella looked at her and said that she didn't understand it. She had urinated all over the floor. Enzo looked at his mother who then wailed.

"Get the midwife," she screamed at Enzo. "It's coming!"

The midwife, an old crone that everyone called Mama Fucilla, arrived an hour later. She was having dinner with her half-sister when Enzo came to her door. She let him in, but her dinner would not be disturbed. After confirming that there was no bleeding or excessive pain, she returned to eating. Enzo paced and paced in the midwife's living room, not understanding the lack of urgency on the part of Mama Fucilla. When she was done, she put on her shawl, grabbed her valise of essentials and told Enzo to lead the way. The rain had by now subsided to a drizzle.

They arrived at Enzo's house drenched. The rain began again, this time with a vengeance. They found Gabriella pacing the floor, with Signora Vespucci by her side. The midwife told Enzo to dry himself then boil some water and to get clean cloths. Mama Fucilla then proceeded to ask Gabriella some questions. Despite the pain, she answered as best she could. The midwife and her mother-in-law helped her make her way to the bed. She was told to push and push. Signora Vespucci told her to push some more. Gabriella pushed for what seemed like an eternity. Then, she felt like she was being torn in two. Finally at 2 am, on June 16, 1805, Gabriella delivered a baby boy. The midwife cleaned and wrapped the baby, handing it to Signora Vespucci, who was beaming with unparalleled joy.

Enzo heard the baby cry from outside the bedroom door. He wept overtly, knowing that the baby was safe. Then it was quiet. Too quiet. He waited a few more minutes then knocked softly. A harsh voice came from within, stating that they were not finished. There was still another one on its way.

Another one!

The birth of the twins caused a minor sensation in the neighborhood. Although not highly unusual, the event was seen as good luck for the family and the town. The phenomenon was the source of much speculation among the womenfolk who had their own hypothesis on how this came to be. The causes of conceiving twins became a rather important topic that June. A few speculated that Gabriella had eaten a fruit, say like an orange. Many had noticed that oranges sometimes may have a smaller orange growing out of it. Maybe she ate that. A few were of the belief that she had prayed to St. Benedict, who was St. Scholastica's twin. There were many visitors dropping by the Vespucci household that whole month, all the way till the end of July. By August though, the novelty faded. Another reason was that a farmer's cow in the nearby city of Siena had given birth to a calf with two heads.

When the time came to baptize the boys, Enzo and Gabrielle were pressed to come up with names. *'Catarina'* was out. You simply didn't change it to *'Catarino'*. Annunziata was out. Signora Vespucci suggested the masculine form, Nunzio, for the older one. Nunzio, however, was Secunda's father's name, and Enzo thought it highly inappropriate, not to mention the fact that Enzo detested the man and didn't want him boasting to anyone that one of the twins was named after him.

After much deliberation, the couple (and even Enzo's mother agreed) they would call the older one Giaochinno, after Enzo's grandfather. Signora Vespucci was pleased. The younger one would be named Vincenzo, after Gabriella's own maternal grandfather, who was a decorated war hero and philosopher. Signora Vespucci was not too thrilled, but then Gabriella explained the other reason. She said it was similar to, phonetically speaking, Lorenzo's name. Enzo was, after all named after Signora Vespucci's husband, Lorenzo senior, who died when the boy was still an infant.

The boys were baptized at the Cathedral of San Gimignano. Little did anyone know that the very church where they received their first sacrament would be the starting point of their difficult journey.

The boys grew. At the age of two, they were speaking their native language fluently. Enzo, so used to being doted on by his mother and wife, was unhappy on his new, lesser position. By some strange reasoning, he resented the constant affection Annunziata lavished on them. He took exception to Gabriella spending too much time with them, while he labored and slaved away. Oddly, he subconsciously saw his sons as contenders for the love of his women. With this seed planted firmly in his heart, the branches of resentment grew. It was at this time that Enzo began to spend more time at the tavern again.

Their grandmother constantly showed them off, although she was slightly disappointed that they weren't girls. She would take them out in a wooden cart that she had a carpenter custom build for her. She would dress them alike when she went to visit her friends who fussed over the adorable toddlers. One envious grandmother said superciliously that they weren't identical, but fraternal. Grandmother Vespucci looked at the woman and told her that at least her son wasn't a *finocchio.* The woman gasped as Grandmother Vespucci turned away and left. Finocchio was Italian for homosexual.

When the boys turned five, Gabriella got pregnant again. Annunziata was certain that this time, it would be a girl. Enzo, whose disposition had slowly worsened was not as pleased. He began to complain how bad enough it was to feed two children, now they had another on the way. Enzo also began to gamble. He was not working as much, losing workdays due to his drinking. Gabriella, tired of nagging him to go to work, found herself working again, taking in washing and selling fish once more. Money was scarce. If not for Grandmother Vespucci, the family would have starved. She always had foresight in economic matters, most especially when Enzo's father died suddenly long ago. Left with a little money, she slaved and put aside money for her old age. When it had reached a sizeable portion, she looked for creative ways to reinvest.

One of those ways was to lend it to people in need, with a slightly high interest of course. This is what kept mother and child alive all that time. When Enzo reached manhood, she had stopped this business of credit.

Now, once again, Grandmother Vespucci started lending out money.

Enzo got into fights. He argued constantly with his mother and Gabriella. He also began to physically hit the boys for the tiniest of errors. Because of this, Annunziata or Gabriella never left the boys alone with their father. One evening, he arrived home drunk, demanding money to buy more liquor. Gabriella told him to go to sleep, but he went straight for the jar where the money for the household expenses was kept. Gabriella stopped him from taking it. She didn't care if she starved, but her children would have at least some milk and one square meal a day. It was then that Enzo hit her for the very first time. He slapped her hard. Then slapped her again, calling her names. The twins, woken by their loud arguing, came in to see their father abusing their mother. They started crying. Enzo turned to hit one of them, but Gabriella rushed to protect them. Enzo hit her again and again. Vincenzo howled even louder as Giaochinno started pummeling his father with his tiny fists. Enzo punched Gabriella and she fell, hitting her head hard against the kitchen table. She would have that half-moon scar on the left side of her forehead for the rest of her life.

Annunziata, who was about to change into her nightgown, rushed out of her bedroom to see what the commotion was all about. Gabriella was on the floor still clutching the jar, the twins beside her.

Enzo flung Giaochinno aside. He then grabbed

Vincenzo, who hung on to his mother for dear life. With Vincenzo out of the way, Enzo kicked her swollen stomach and Gabriella screamed in agony.

That was enough for Signora Vespucci. In one clear moment, she saw the error of her ways, the times she defended this man-child, justified his bad behavior, reasoned his anger. She grabbed the nearest thing she could find, a twelve inch plaster statue of the Virgin Mary which she had had for many years. She raised it and smashed it over Enzo's head. Enzo fell to the floor, dazed but uninjured. Annunziata screamed at him, cursed him and ordered him to leave. On his knees, Enzo started to weep.

Annunziata quieted the twins and comforted Gabriella, who sobbed inconsolably. She brought Gabriella and the boys to her room and tucked them in, whispering words of comfort. When the twins finally fell asleep and Gabriella's weeping quieted to a few whimpers here and there, she went to sweep the remnants of the religious figure. Enzo was nowhere to be found. Signora Vespucci found the jar on the floor, opened. It was empty.

Chapter 7

Gabriella lost her baby. Something that she would never forgive Enzo for until her dying day. Still, her grief was assuaged by her two boys, who comforted her, made her laugh when she was sad. They adored her, and she them.

By the age of seven, the boys were precocious and charming. They were passably well-behaved as any seven year old could be. They were also small in stature, looking far younger than their stated age. They didn't play with the other boys as much, finding their own company sufficient. They were also deeply afraid of their father, but would valiantly engage him in conversation, try to do small things for him, in the hope that one day their love would save him from this affliction and the impenetrable wall he had put up.

Grandmother Vespucci and Gabriella took them to mass at San Bartolo every Sunday. Sometimes, a Bishop would visit and say High mass, which was at the time sung in Latin. It was after such a mass that the twins displayed their true talents.

It was suppertime and Gabriella, Annunziata and the twins were getting ready to eat. Enzo as usual, was absent. The four made the sign of the cross. Then Annunziata took the lead to say grace. When she was finished, the two women said 'Amen'. The twins, however, as if pre-planned, launched into a short but complex, two-part amen. Grandmother Vespucci clapped her hands, impressed by such talent, while Gabriella laughed and hugged both of them. *Amen* was fine, they said, but how about any other songs. Vincenzo then stood up and said in a singsong manner; *In nominee Patris et Filii et Spiritus Sancti* and once again ended it with an Amen. After that, grandmother and mother encouraged them to learn a few more songs.

"But we know lots of songs," Vincenzo said. Giaochinno then sang the opening lines of '*Sebben crudele.*' Vincenzo joined him, putting in some of his counterpoint. The two women were short of astounded. When they realized that the two were waiting for some kind of reaction from them, both mother and Grandmother lavished them with praises. Annunziata hugged both her grandchildren, calling them angels and other terms of endearment. Gabriella covered them with kisses and added whatever grandmother may have left off.

If their mother and grandmother reprimanded them for that, or if they did not give such abundant praise, hugs and kisses, perhaps it would have been different. Music to them would be something dishonorable and shameful. But the positive reaction of the two women they both loved very much made music what it truly is; a gift. A gift which required nothing in return, but to be received wholehearted and openly.

The twins began to devour their dinners, talking excitedly between mouthfuls about how Signora Conti from next door sang *Sebben Crudele* over and over again that they learned it. Signora Conti was abandoned by her husband to join the war and he never returned. She still pined for him, hoping that he wasn't dead, but would one day come back.

One day, as Signora Conti hung her wash outside, she began to sing the song again. The boys, who were playing nearby, approached her. She did not see them, she was at the time pinning a large, freshly washed bed sheet. When she began to sing the refrain, the boys joined her. She was at first astounded. She pushed away the sheet to find the two little boys smiling at her. She laughed and laughed. She asked them if they knew any other songs. Not many, they replied. Well, Signora Conti took it upon herself to teach them a few more.

Gabriella and Annunziata listened to their tale with wonder. They couldn't eat, but watched the children in surprise and gratitude. While the twins rambled on about this and that, Gabriella and Annunziata's heads were churning with thoughts and ideas on how to develop what truly was such a God-given talent.

When supper was over, the dishes cleared and the twins put to bed, Annunziata and Gabriella set to the task of discussing the twin's future. There was no doubt that they were endowed with something special. But how to cultivate it? Annunziata smiled and told Gabriella that she knew exactly what to do. Gabriella was curious as to why Annunziata seemed so confident, so she told Gabriella to sit so she could tell the story better.

Ever since the older Signora Vespucci started lending out money again, she was privy to a lot of information of what was happening around town. She began to recount to Gabriella how she was the first to hear of this and that. Gabriella, trying not to be rude, prodded her to get back with how this was going to help them.

Miffed at not being allowed to paint her self-importance, Annunziata nevertheless told her how she heard of a refined gentleman who lived right in San Gimignano. His marvelous town house located at the Via San Mateo. Rudolfo Santussi was his name, was well known in court, for he was indeed a *'Maestro di Musica'*, a professor of music and vocal coach. It was rumored that the *maestro* had even studied under the likes of Muzio Clementi and Domenico Scarlatti. Names that didn't matter to Annunziata, but she was still impressed. All that mattered was that people spoke well of him. She had forgotten all about it until today. They decided that they would bring the twins to this Santussi. Surely, such a man of brilliance would discern the talent the twins possessed immediately.

The next day, Annunziata started their chores earlier than usual. When the morning chores were done, Gabriella bathed the boys. Annunziata dressed them in their Sunday best. The boys asked where were they going. It wasn't Sunday. Why were they so dressed up? Their grandmother told them that they were going to town to meet a very important and great man.

"Who is he, Mama?" Vincenzo asked, always the cautious one.

"He is a very intelligent man who knows all about singing and music." Gabriella brushed his hair.

"Maybe Vincenzo and I could sing *amen* for him." Giaochinno volunteered.

The two women smiled at each other. They saw that there would be no problem in getting these two to perform.

When they were ready, Gabriella wrote and left a note on the kitchen table for Enzo, who came in very late the night before and was still in bed, in all likelihood in a drunken stupor.

The trek to town was not too arduous. The day was cool, despite the bright sunshine, and a soft breeze accompanied them all the way to town. The boys laughed and chased each other, but was warned by Gabriella not to, lest they soiled their good clothes. A mile down the road, the had to make way and walk on the side of the narrow dirt road for a small caravan of traveling players and troubadours, headed the opposite way.

"Who are they, mama?" Giaochinno asked. Gabriella told the boys they were players who put on comic plays. Some juggled and danced. They also sang songs and played instruments, performing for people in other towns. The better ones even performed for royalty, or the Pope. These ones were paid handsomely.

Giaochinno announced that when he grew up, he too would travel all over the world to perform and get paid handsomely to do so.

"Me, too!" Vincenzo piped in.

Annunziata made the sign of the cross, spit once and muttered audibly, "From your mouth to God's ears, my little ones."

They arrived a little after ten o'clock. They entered the town through the Gate of San Giovanni, a peculiar arch erected in the 12th century that was miraculously still preserved. The gate led them to Via San Giovanni, one of the main thoroughfares of the city. They walked some more and the women made a sign of the cross when they passed a brickwork building with mullioned windows. This was the *Palazzo Pratellesi,* which used to be a nunnery and therefore, a holy place.

When they reached *Piazza della Cisterna,* or the Cistern Square, so named because of a large cistern well located there, Annunziata had to stop. She cursed her age and told Gabriella to give her a chance to breathe. The boys by now grabbed their mother's hand and began to pull her towards the *Confetteria Dulce*. The store had been recently opened, much to the delight of the townsfolk. One quick glance at its window displayed all manners of confectionary delight. Spicy candy, chocolates, lemon sugar and *marroni* (chestnuts) were exhibited in various guises. While the boys 'oohed' and 'aahed' loudly, Gabriella wondered at the kind of people that came in to buy such luxuries. Annunziata, finally catching her breath, joined the three by the window. Ever the doting grandmother, she promised the twins that if they behaved, they could return later in the afternoon to pick up some penny candy.

Via San Mateo was lined with the most beautiful and very well preserved medieval mansions, many of them residences of the more affluent citizens of San Gimignano. Although they knew that the maestro lived on this street, they weren't sure which of the imposing structures his house was. Gabriella stopped a well-dressed man and begging his pardon asked if she knew where the great maestro Rudolfo Santussi lived. The man graciously informed them that they were standing right in front of it, and pointed behind them.

The women turned and were immediately intimidated. The building, aside from its significant height and breadth was constructed in an elegant low renaissance style. Gabriella turned around to thank the man, leaving Annunziata to wonder at the cost of having such a mansion. The man smiled, said *prego* and continued his stroll.

They made their way up the stone steps. Annunziata grasped the ornate knocker, a large affair of a brass ring caught in a lion's mouth. She brought the knocker down three times, somewhat forcefully. They waited. Gabriella was about to suggest trying the knocker again when the locking mechanism from the other side gave a loud click. The massive oak door opened slightly, revealing a quizzical looking, emaciated bald man in a waist coat.

"Maestro Santussi?" Annunziata smiled.

"The Maestro is busy."

Annunziata frowned. This man wasn't the maestro. But of course! A man of his stature wouldn't answer his own door, she thought. This had to be his manservant.

"We've come to see the maestro, please" she smiled again, with a little less cheerfulness.

"The maestro does not see anyone without an appointment" the skeletal excuse of a man said contemptuously.

"Appointment?" Gabriella inquired.

"No, we don't need an appointment. Just a few moments with the maestro." Annunziata pleaded. What did they need with all this formality?

The undernourished valet rolled his eyes, mentioned that if they needed to see the maestro, it was best that they put it in writing. He would deliver it and they would be summoned, if the maestro had time. When the bald man finished delivering these instructions, he wished them good day and proceeded to close the door. Annunziata, quick thinking person that she was, lodged her foot on the threshold thereby thwarting the man's intention to close the door.

"Signor," Annunziata begged, "just a few minutes."

"Si, por favore. We need his advice," Gabrielle added.

They implored, entreated and begged, all the while

trying to push the door open while the waist coated man on the other side repeatedly told the Signora to allow him to close the door. Frankly, he had never encountered such rude women, and despite his training in civility, was beginning to lose his patience.

"Cos'è successo?" A voice from within called. "What is happening here?"

The man froze. Finding his voice, he answered that there were some persistent women at the door without an appointment.

"Open the door, please, Angelo" the voice said.

"*Si*, Maestro."

When the door was finally opened, the twins looked up to see an extremely tall man, taller than their father, taller than anyone they've ever met. He was elegantly dressed in a smoking jacket of brocade cloth. A large handle bar mustache dominated the wrinkled face. Although the maestro was well into his seventies, his demeanor and carriage belied his true age. He was indeed, very dignified.

"Maestro," Annunziata gave a slight curtsy. Gabriella followed suit.

"And what may I do for you, Signora--?"

"Signora Vespucci, Maestro." Annunziata then began to tell him of their visit.

Santussi invited them in and ordered his manservant to bring in some refreshments for his guests. Angelo, maintaining decorum, left to comply with his master's wishes, even though he reflected on the quality of his company, specifically the older woman.

Maestro Santussi listened to the women and asked the boys to sing. When they were finished, he contemplated the talent in front of him. The boys' tone, to his trained ear, was one of clarity and purity. The fact that both voices possessed the same qualities, why, what were the odds of that? He was astonished and he prided himself on not easily being astonished.

The twins were truly gifted, no doubt about it. With a little training, they would go very far. That was, until they reached puberty and their voice broke. God only knows what they would sound like then.

The women looked at him expectantly. He knew that these women could ill afford music lessons. Neither did he have the inclination, since he had made his mind up that he was now retired, not to mention that he only worked with adults. Still, there was one option. An elegant option in fact, one that would benefit everyone.

He had dined recently with the Monsignor who mentioned that a certain Father Russo would be starting a choir for boys. Father Russo had come from Milan. The Archbishop thought him highly competent in all matters musical. Yes, Santussi had indeed heard of this priest. He tried to recall when the auditions were supposed to be: Friday. It would be next Friday. But that was the previous week when the Monsignor and he last saw each other. He thought about it then realized that today was the day. "Angelo!" he cried. "The carriage!"

When they arrived at the Cathedral, there were boys everywhere. Boys playing hide and seek, boys playing marbles. Some people had set up blankets to sit on, others had brought stools and chairs. A group was playing cards. There was a festive mood in the air as entire families picnicked on the steps of the church.

They alighted from the carriage and made straight for

the doorway, as the adults scrutinized the maestro and the small entourage which accompanied him. Many came by horse drawn carts, or buggies. Some by foot. But none of them were that wealthy to have such an opulent conveyance. The arrival of such a man raised an eyebrow or two.

Santussi told the driver not to wait, he would just walk back. They walked up the steps, winding their way through the people. When they got to the door, they spied a crude sign that said something about parents not accompanying their children, which the maestro disregarded. He flung open the door, and found no one in the sanctuary. Well not really no one. There was an adolescent altar boy wiping down a pew.

Francesco looked up and saw the maestro. The maestro needed to speak to Father Russo. Francesco told the tall gentleman that they had just missed the priest by a few minutes, as he had gone to lunch somewhere in town. Francesco saw the boys and asked the maestro if they were here for the auditions. Of course that is why they were here, fumed the maestro. Francesco then asked for the boy's last name. Annunziata answered "Vespucci", whereupon Francesco said that children whose last name beginning with the letter 'V' would be seen between 3 and 5. The maestro thought about it for a while, then asked the boys if they were hungry. They brightened up immediately and answered in the positive. The Maestro asked the altar boy if there was a decent *trattoria* nearby and was given directions to one just across the street. He thanked Francesco and escorted his group out, telling them to follow him. They made their way across the piazza and found the restaurant. He opened the door for the ladies, who promptly told him that this was an expensive place, and were embarrassed to admit that they didn't have much money. The Maestro told them not to worry. The boys were quiet, taking it all in. This was the first time they had been in a restaurant. The maestro asked Annunziata and Gabriella if they had any preference, some chicken perhaps? Gabriella blushed, while Annunziata fanned herself. The waiter came and the maestro ordered for all of them. It was a wonderful luncheon, Santussi being the perfect host, putting the women at ease. He found the twins delightful, who in return thought him funny and engaging, so unlike their father.

The maestro paid the bill, putting Gabriella ill at ease as Annunziata offered to pay for their share. The maestro put on an air of mock alarm, stating that he would be honored if the ladies allowed him to be the gentleman that he was, and permit him to pay. The ladies thanked him profusely. The twins, picking up the cue, hugged the legs of the gentleman and said "*grazie, Maestro*" in concert, which prompted Santussi to scoop both of them in his arms, all three roaring with laughter and pleasure.

When Santussi put the twins down, he said to Annunziata and Gabriella that he wouldn't go with them. The talent of the boys would assure them a place in the choir. Annunziata began to protest, but the maestro explained that the boys' abilities would assure them a position, that his being there would make Father Russo uncomfortable. It would be unethical. The ladies tried not to look too discouraged. Santussi finally, in conclusion, mentioned the plain fact that people talked. He didn't want the old wags whose sons' failed the auditions to gossip or complain about his influence and negate the true talent the boys. Annunziata nodded in assent, knowing the malicious habits of the womenfolk. So after saying their farewells, the four of them made their way back to the Cathedral. The twins waved goodbye. Santussi waved back, smiling contentedly while thinking to himself how music made all men equal, whether they be male or female, giants or midgets.

Chapter 8

For the longest time, the people of San Gimignano feared that Napoleon and his army would one day show up at their front door. By then, Northern Italy was overrun by the French and conditions were precarious. However, in April of 1814, Napoleon had abdicated and the anxiety that many felt began to wane. Things were indeed looking better.

In the Vespucci household however, things had gotten worse. The preliminary excitement of the boys' acceptance to Father Russo's choir had begun to diminish. The boys were evidently very diligent in attending rehearsals, which made Enzo even more aggravated. Enzo, if ever around, was increasingly verbal with all four of them, complaining of everything and anything, specifically the boys worthlessness with chores around the house. He viewed music as a useless pastime. The boys should be helping with chores instead of singing. When he was at home, the boys walked on eggshells, since the slightest provocation resulted in a slap or a rap upside the head. Many times, Gabriella or Annunziata had to stop Enzo from physically abusing the boys. He claimed that punishment was good for them. Gabriella claimed that punishment was spanking, not beating them till they were black and blue.

One day, while Annunziata was preparing dinner, she felt a strange tightening on her chest. She fell and from then on began to stay in bed more. She had had a stroke. Gabriella had to work doubly hard, leaving early and coming home late, barely catching the boys before bedtime. She would spend a few minutes with them, time and again saying she loved them and that the reason she couldn't be there all the time should be plain enough.

Annunziata took a turn for the worse. She had another stroke, leaving her half-paralyzed. Enzo, filled with fear, swore to the Virgin of the Immaculate Conception that he would never again touch a drop of liquor if the Queen of Heaven would heal his mother. He started looking for work again. Finding work was difficult though, since he had developed a reputation for being unreliable.

Whenever he was not out seeking employment, he would help around the house, chopping wood, hauling water and helping Annunziata with her chores. Despite her fractional paralysis, Annunziata stubbornly refused to be bedridden. She still managed to cook the meals for the family, despite Enzo's protestations for her to slow down. With Gabriella gone and Annunziata bedridden, the twins helped around the house as much as they could. But whatever they did, Enzo found fault with them and would beat them with a stick or his hands. He told them that they were useless. The beatings in fact seemed forthcoming whenever they came from choir practice. How could they still be engaged in this stupid singing while their grandmother hobbled around? He roared at them.

Annunziata (and Gabriella, when she was around) defended the twins singing, which increased Enzo's indignation. Enzo also learned to lambaste Father Russo, hinting that there was something wrong with a man like that. What was wrong? Well, just look at him, a man who dabbled in music, who liked the company of young boys. Surely Father Russo was an *'omosessuale'*. Wasn't it obvious? Both the ladies were shocked at such an accusation. Father Russo was a man of God! They begged him not to speak ill of this man of the cloth, lest God smite him and send him to hell.

Father Russo had trained his choir passionately for the past two years. At first he started with simpler pieces, and given the impressionability of the young minds, they quickly learned. He then proceeded to teach the boys more complex pieces. By the summer of 1814, he would allow the choir to perform pieces from Johann Sebastian Bach's Mass in B Minor, which had taken them a few months to work on. It was perfect timing. It soon would be the festival of Santa Fina, the patron saint of San Gimignano. It was to be a grand affair, with the Cathedral playing host to a multitude of activities.

This year, such an illustrious list of guests like his mentor, the Archbishop of Milan and Cardinal Firrao, who was representing Pope Pius VII, would be there. Cardinal Firrao in fact, was officiating the high mass. Father Russo didn't much care for the other guests, persons of wealth and royalty, who were far more popular and admired, simply because they were, to him, unspiritual. The church would be overflowing that day, he thought. Father Russo encouraged the boys that that day their performance would certainly be "*Ad maioren Dei gloriam,*" to the greater glory of God.

Music for the mass would be a grand affair with different pieces of music gracing the event. A few of pieces, parts from Bach's Mass in B minor, whom many in music considered to be Bach's "*opus ultimum*", would be the main attraction.

The organ was tuned, and a small orchestra (through the graciousness of the Papal office who supplied the funds) had been assembled. A harpsichord was brought all the way from Milan, again, courtesy of the Archbishop.

Father Russo had already chosen who would sing the lead in the vocally complex *"Domine Deus."* The Domine Deus was really a duet that was sung right before the *"Credo".* The duet, many music lovers were apt to agree, was an emphasis on the relationship of God the Father and Christ the Son. The piece would start with a playful flute and violin duet, playing the theme. Then the tenor (an accomplished tenor from Sicily whom Father Russo had employed) would sing *"Domine Deus"* which of course was speaking of the Father. The soprano would enter, singing "*Domine Fili,*" speaking of the son. The tenor and soprano lines playfully interlaced and finally, at the very end of the duet, both tenor and soprano sing the last parts of the text together. Giaochinno Vespucci would sing the soprano part.

Father Russo was certain that when Bach composed this particular piece, he had intended a boy soprano and a male tenor to sing. Not a female soprano! (How blasphemous! he reviled at the thought.)

After the mass, as the cardinal, archbishop and monsignor exited, the boys stood still. It would not do for them to exit in a rowdy fashion, in respect to the Cardinal and the other dignitaries. They stood still, until all that was left was the majority of female church-goers, who stayed a little to gawk at the beautiful clothes of the high born ladies.

Finally, after what seemed hours, the boys exited in an orderly fashion. When they got to the anteroom however, they started to whisper among each other about what note they missed, who missed their cue, and how they wish they could sing like their Giaochinno, who put the tenor to shame.

Father Russo came in as they were changing. He clapped his hands and said they should be proud of themselves. He told Giaochinno and Vincenzo that it was too bad that their mother couldn't make it, (Gabriella had been in bed for the last week, sick with dysentery) the boys were more relaxed and now spoke excitedly among themselves.

Just then, the door slammed open. Enzo came in, looking wild. He had been drinking again. The boys hushed. The priest asked who he was.

"I am the father of those two!" he spat, pointing to Giaochinno and Vincenzo. The boys felt their faces grow hot. This was, perhaps the most embarrassing moment in their life.

"Go home!" Enzo shouted at them.

"Signor Vespucci. Please, you do not have to scream."

"I can do what I want," He looked at Father Russo with slits for eyes.

Father Russo didn't want a scene, but he didn't want the boys to leave with this man either, not like this. Father Russo, though not a man of violence, was ready to defend his boys if need be, and readied himself for a fight. As if on cue, the Monsignor came in with a party of men and a couple of women.

"Ah, Father Russo, you must be full of pride," The Archbishop smiled wide. By his side was an obese man richly dressed.

"Father Russo, I think you have met Signor Conte Gaspari."

"Your lordship," the priest bowed slightly.

"Your boys should be pleased with how they carried

out their task," Gaspari wheezed, as he wiped his perspiring brow with a lace handkerchief.

"You are most kind, your lordship," replied the priest.

"Most especially the little one who sang the Domine" his eyes focused on Giaochinno.

"Ah yes, he is our *vox principalis,*" the Monsignor interjected.

"Such an angelic face, Emanuele," one of the women in the company walked towards him and caressed his cheek.

"Just look at him," the lady continued, "like a little angel."

"He has a brother…" Enzo exclaimed. "A twin."

"Ah yes, Vincenzo, come here." Father Russo called to the little boy. Vincenzo had managed to hide behind a larger boy during his father's ranting. He stepped out in front. Father Russo realized he was now caught in a bind. To not introduce the twin's father would be rude, but surely Enzo wouldn't cross such personage.

"Your grace, your lordship, permit me to introduce Lorenzo Vespucci, their father."

Perhaps Enzo was cowed to be in such company. He looked at Father Russo, who met his gaze and pointed to his ring finger. Enzo quickly realized what the priest was telling him, and he went on his knees to kiss the archbishop's ring.

"Your grace." He said, remembering his catechism. He stood and bowed to Gaspari and said *"Mi piacere,* your excellency." Which made a few in the crowd titter. 'Your excellency' was a title used for bishops. Father Russo began talking about the next musical performance, answering questions from the assembled. As the crowd began to talk amongst themselves about the exceptional music they would soon be hearing, Gaspari studied the man the twins called their father. How could two beautiful vessels come from this jar of clay?

Il Conte Gaspari was a lover of beauty. Unexpectedly, he felt compelled to address the unkempt man who smelled of liquor.

"You must be very proud, Signor Vespucci."

"You cannot eat pride, your eminence." Enzo said.

Gaspari would have been shocked at the presumptuous tone used, but he would tolerate it, for now.

"The boys, they have a great future ahead of them."

"As you say, your lordship." Vespucci answered neutrally. "In fact, I used to sing also, but I had to give it up to work."

"Let me be so bold as to say that I would like to help them in their pursuit of music. Do you know the Palazzo di Cardinale?" Gaspari asked nonchalantly. Enzo nodded.

"Be there tomorrow morning, at nine o'clock. We shall talk." And with that Gaspari turned around and left Enzo wondering.

When the dignitaries left, Enzo roughly grabbed the two boys and dragged them out. Father Russo followed them as far as the door, watching the three make their way down the street.

The priest shook his head. "Watch over them", he intoned to the Virgin. He felt quite ill. It wasn't fear, he knew that. He realized that for the first time in his life, he felt hatred. Malice was in his heart as he silently prayed for forgiveness, all the while thinking that Vespucci was a very evil man.

That same night, at the Palazzo di Cardinale, the very same people who congratulated Father Russo were having dinner. The dinner was superb, with the Cardinal's personal cook overseeing the banquet. The Cardinal, ever an efficient host, made sure that his guests were well fed and well entertained. The meal was simply abundant. Hors d'oeuvres and delicate French-style soups were followed by a dazzling array of meat and fish dishes, vegetable purees, intricate sweets and fruit --all carried in by liveried servants and presented with extreme attention to detail.

A string quartet had been engaged while they supped, and later there would be fireworks. The Conte, used to such culinary display, pretended to be awed. Still, he only played with his *filetto di maiale con castraure* (pork fillet with baby artichokes.) Despite the supreme efforts of the cooking staff, the Count did not have much of an appetite. Something was bothering him, but he couldn't identify it. The conversation turned to the astounding sound of the young choir. One of the younger ladies said that the twins were so adorable, looking like little angels. The Cardinal began to launch into a soliloquy about the history of choir music, beginning with Gregorian chant. Gaspari tried to redirect his grace back to the original subject. Another gentleman, a French viscount whose name escaped Gaspari, interjected that he had been to Rome recently and had heard a similar choir, but they wouldn't hold a candle to the excellence he found in San Gimignano. Immediately, the Count's spirits lifted. He realized what had bothered him, and that his wealth would be able to fix it.

Chapter 9

Il Conte Emanuele Gaspari never knew what it was like to be hungry or poor. The son of Il Conte Massimo Giuliano Gaspari and the Contessa Maria Melino, little Emanuele had everything, literally. For one, he had wealth. The Gaspari family could trace back their lineage back one hundred years. They were even, to some extent, related to the House of Savoy. Massimo, Emanuele's father, had inherited a massive amount of wealth, properties and holdings when his father had died. Massimo went ahead and re-invested all he could into the commerce of the era, having the foresight to invest in all manners of industries. When Emanuele was born, Massimo had already quadrupled the family's net worth, which was already substantial to begin with.

Massimo and Maria tried very hard to have children, but after two miscarriages, the prognosis was dismal. She would never have any children.

The Conte may have been resigned to that, but the Contessa was another matter. She consulted doctors, midwives and any other person that may have some solution to her reported barrenness. Finally, after years of trying, she finally got pregnant.

Emanuele was an only child. The Contessa loved him dearly and spoiled him. He was thoroughly overprotected and was never allowed to be alone. Emanuele grew to be a stubborn child, never doing what he was told. He stomped around Palazzo Gaspari, constantly annoying the help. Since he was, after all, the count-to-be, no one ever reprimanded him. Nanny after nanny was hired and quit, all of them trying very hard to correct him. Each constantly reported to the Contessa about her darling *"Ficuccio"* (literally meaning "little fig") and his exploits. The Contessa would in turn tell the governess that 'boys would be boys' or 'he'll grow out of it' or some other justification to his bad behavior.

Like any child in such a household, he was privately tutored. His first tutor, a certain scholar from France lasted barely a month. A quick succession of other educators and pedagogues entered and exited the Palazzo. The Gasparis were of the belief that Europe was sadly lacking in good educators, even though deep down, they didn't believe it. Finally, when the boy had just turned eleven years of age, a monk by the name of Fra Domenico was referred to them by the good monsignor of their parish. They sent for him immediately. When he arrived, he cloistered himself with the parents of the boy and laid down his conditions. The boy's education was solely his concern and responsibility. He was strict and he believed in conferring punishment to modify poor manners, but was fair about it. The Conte and Contessa were shocked at his effrontery and considered sending him packing. Then the good friar told them the truth, that without consequences or boundaries, he would grow up wild and immoral. If that was what they had wanted for their only child, then so be it, he would leave immediately.

They had been defeated. They were told what they knew deep down but would never own up to. Fra Domenico proceeded to explain the loss of heaven and the pains of hell. When he had their complete attention, he advanced from the spiritual to the physical, lecturing them on the corporeal afflictions of immorality that made the

Contessa partly swoon and the Count feel ill. The monk then asked for their pronouncement. The frightened parents could do nothing but agree to his conditions.

The potential pairing of the ascetic monk and the riotous child became the subject of petty betting in the Gaspari household. The servants all took a pool on when the monk would leave. The first day was excluded in the pool; mostly all had wanted it. The major-domo of the house was given first choice. He immediately took the second day. No one had wanted the thirtieth day, which would have meant a whole month, for no one had ever stayed that long. Then the scullery maid (who in any household was paid and treated the worst) had faith in God and in this Fra Domenico. He was a holy man, none of the other teachers were. She said she would take the thirtieth day. She also put forth that she should be promptly paid the money on the thirty-first day. They all laughed at her, but agreed.

Fra Domenico was what the boy needed. He was honest, compassionate and strict. More importantly, he didn't need the job and couldn't be threatened with unemployment, bodily harm or mental aggravation. When they first met, Fra Domenico told the boy that he would not tolerate any foolishness and that he would be punished for being slothful or disrespectful. That same night, Emanuele stole into Fra Domenico's room and cut the monk's hair as he slept (not that there was much to cut, the monk already had a tonsure.) When he saw his teacher the next day, the monk started with his lessons, completely unmindful that his head was bare. Emanuele pointed it out, hoping to vex the monk, who remained unimpassioned.

Emanuele did not pay attention to the lesson that day, which was on Latin verbs. Instead, he feigned illness, stating that he had a headache. Fra Domenico said that he would either complete the lesson or suffer the consequence. Emanuele impudently pretended fear. None of his teachers ever dared to punish him. Fra Domenico got up quickly and grabbed the boy. Before Emanuele could even cry for help, the monk had him placed on his lap, his derriere up in the air. The monk spanked him once, twice, up to a dozen times. The boy got up, screamed at the monk and promised him that he was going to tell the Contessa that his person was harmed.

The boy ran to his mother's room. Rubbing his buttocks, he wheezed that Fra Domenico tried to kill him. The Contessa wrung her kerchief and asked her maid to summon the monk to the outer salon. The boy sat down, expectant. His mother took her seat and waited. When Fra Domenico arrived, she smiled uneasily and asked if it was true that he tried to, ah, kill her son. The monk looked at her and said that this would not do. He could not perform his task if the boy was allowed to run in here every time he was punished for his misdeeds. Fra Domenico began his litany again of the things that the wicked would sow if their path were not straightened. He begged her leave and thanked her for her hospitality. She stood up and said in a small voice that Emanuele was not a bad child. He looked at her and stated that no, he was not a bad child. He was punished for his bad behavior. She looked at Emanuele and asked him if he was disrespectful. He whined that he was not, that Fra Domenico was a monster. She got down on his level and grasped both his shoulders and told him that he would apologize to his teacher, lest he receive the same retribution from her. Emanuele was stunned. He slowly walked up to the monk and said *"Fra Domenico. Por favore, sono spiacente.* I am very sorry."

"I did not punish you because you are a bad boy. You are a good boy, with bad habits. We will get rid of the bad habits and replace them with good ones." The monk left. The Contessa left. Emanuele sat all alone in the salon for a long time, plotting revenge.

The next day, Emanuele got up early and when to the stables. He coerced the stable boy to carry a bag of horse manure to the monk's room. The monk had opposed to sleeping in the upper part of the house, whose guest bedrooms' were too opulent for his tastes. (He was after all, still bound by the rules of his order.) Instead, he appealed to have a room in the basement, where most of the servants' quarters were located, and chose the most austere one. His bed was a wooden pallet, with a straw mattress. Emanuele ordered the stable boy to stuff the mattress with the manure. Although the stable boy was hesitant, he knew better than to cross the young master's wishes. When the deed was done, Emanuele told the stable boy not to speak to anyone about it, lest he wanted to lose his job. Gleefully, he returned to eat breakfast. When the time came for him to meet with his tutor, he feigned diligence, applying himself to the academic matters at hand, pleasing Fra Domenico who honestly thought that there would be no more hooliganism.

Fortunately, the stable boy told the stable master, who told the housekeeper who told the major-domo who in turn warned the monk. The monk thanked him, and had the young lout summoned to his bedroom. After being spanked (this time with a paddle), Emanuele was ordered to take out the offending excrement, adding insult to injury. He was also instructed to fill a new mattress with clean straw.

Every day for a whole fortnight, Emanuele came up with new and imaginative ways to make Fra Domenico's life difficult. Unfortunately, being a spoiled young man, he never ventured to execute his mischief by himself. He always ordered one of the lesser staff to do it for him. The staff meanwhile, tired of his tyranny, never failed to get word to the monk of his plans. By the end of the day, Emanuele could not afford to sit down without some major discomfort. The pranks finally stopped, the monk stayed, and the poor scullery maid found herself the winner of the pool.

Fra Domenico knew that he had won the battle, but not the war. Without redirecting the boy's energy to something positive, his susceptibility to returning to his ways would be a surety. He needed some leverage. The boy, however, had no passion for anything. Till one day he noticed Emanuele drawing. The boy was totally absorbed, for once. Fra Domenico was still observing him when an idea came to him. He left the boy for a while and proceeded to write a letter. He gave it to the major-domo to dispatch and then waited patiently for a reply. The reply came a few days later. He read it, pleased with the response. He then went to the Conte to ask permission for the boy to go with him to Florence, for a few days to further his education. The Conte agreed and suggested that when in Florence, they could stay with his cousin, an old widower who would enjoy seeing little Emanuele. He would write her of their arrival. Fra Domenico and Emanuele left for Florence the next week.

Despite wanting to start right away on his mission, Fra Domenico was forced to endure at least one day of social graces. Upon arrival at Florence, they paid their respects to the lady, presenting her with a bolt of silk and other gifts from her cousin, the Conte Gaspari. She embraced the boy whom she hadn't seen for two years and invited them to join her for dinner which she had specially prepared for them. During dinner, a quiet affair that involved just the three of them, Fra Domenico found out that their hostess was also a patron of the arts. He remarked that Emanuele was improving scholastically, but needed culture in his life. The grand dame was only so happy to help the boy. She told him that if he needed anything he should just ask. He answered that he would indeed take up the offer.

The next day, the teacher and his student walked to the Via Dei Lamberti. It wasn't too far, and Fra Domenico was a firm believer in exercise. The letter he had written a while back was to a good friend of his, one Signor Giovanni Domenico Tiepolo, who was a well sought after painter.

Tiepolo was only too glad to see his friend. They left Emanuele to watch Tiepolo's assistants ground pigments as they conferred. Fra Domenico laid out his plans to the painter. Tiepolo was only too glad to help. Tiepolo then called Emanuele and asked him if he liked to draw. The boy answered in the affirmative, to which Tiepolo said that painting was drawing, only with color. He then showed the boy a rather large painting that he was working on. He asked him what he thought of it. Emanuele, not one to keep his opinions complained that there were too many people in it. Tiepolo laughed. He then explained who the characters were and why they needed to be there. They boy listened attentively. The master then took an empty canvas, placed a charcoal stick on the boy's hand and told him to sketch on part of the scene, as to how it should look like. Emanuele confidently started drawing.

"No, no," the maestro said. "You need perspective," he then proceeded to tell about foreground and background. As they were discussing all this, Fra Domenico took his rosary and began to pray.

Emanuele spent three intensive days with the master, learning all he can about the rudiments of painting. Fra Domenico was pleased.

They returned to the Palazzo di Gaspari two weeks after. That whole week, Emanuele could not stop talking to his parents, and anyone who listened for that matter about the greatness of the people he had met in Florence. He met three Painters, a sculptor, an architect, a violinist and a tenor. Of all the people he had met, Tiepolo and the tenor, whom he had seen in an *opera comedia* were the two that made the greatest impact on the young mind. Fra Domenico was extremely content. His plan had worked. The boy was now a lover of the arts. He would always fill his world with what was beautiful. The monk thought that with that hunger in him, the boy would devote his energy in trying to fill it.

For a couple of years, Emanuele became an enthusiast, filling his time with painting and composition. The sad part was that the boy showed only a mediocre talent in both fields. As much as he wanted to succeed, he was only second-rate, if at best. His painting were good, but not masterpieces. His singing was adequate, satisfactory, but not outstanding. Perhaps it was his frustration. Perhaps it was his great love for all things beautiful and pleasing and his inability to possess the talent.

Whatever the case may be, Emanuele felt lost and began to eat. He gained weight at an alarming and frightful pace. Fra Domenico encouraged him to eat less and exercise, but all in vain. Unfortunately, Fra Domenico was called back to his monastery, leaving a very heavyset, frustrated and downcast young man of fifteen.

"Do the best you can", he told the boy.

"My best is not good enough." Gaspari hung his head in shame.

"Maybe, but you do have a gift that no one else has." Emanuele looked up, hopeful.

"You have wealth, and you have passion. With those two, you may not possess the talent, but you may encourage it. It will be as if you own it." Fra Domenico left. Emanuele vowed that he would take his tutor's suggestion seriously.

From that day on, Emanuele filled his life with beauty and grace. He invited artists and musicians, commissioning them works. He traveled and bought many fine objects. His father died, leaving him all the Gaspari wealth, which he used to collect more objets d'art.

When he could not buy it, he had it copied. One time, he could not purchase a small, original sculpted piece of marble by Bernini. In love with the beautiful piece, he asked one of the city's foremost sculptor to make a duplicate.

Unfortunately, the duplicate was flawed, ever so slightly, nearly imperceptibly so. To the new Conte's discerning eye however, it was a monstrosity. He destroyed it personally, smashing it. When he could no longer stand it, he had the original stolen. He kept that in his study, away from prying eyes. If caught, he could always say it was a copy. He had the receipt to prove it.

He knew that he should possess only the best, the finest, the purest and the most beautiful. The Vespucci twins were all that. Conte Gaspari was filled with covetousness. Alas, they could not be copied, nor could they be bought. Then again, he knew that everything had a price. Wasn't that what money was for? He reasoned. He continued eating and finished everything on his plate, smiling wickedly.

Chapter 10

The Palazzo di Cardinale was a smaller building located behind the more important Palazzo di Popolo, right in the center of town. It was originally designed by the master Gothic architect Arnolfo di Cambio, who designed Florence's Palazzo Vecchio. However, he died when building began and it was not completed until 1311, under di Cambio's student.

Despite its rich history, many tourists missed it. It seemed only the locals knew of its location. It was tucked away and hidden from the public, much like an idiot child. It had many owners through the years, one family selling it to the next. Finally, in the late 1600's, it was sold to the only buyer in sight; the Roman Catholic Church, who had since kept it.

The church renovated it, pouring a substantial amount in its redecoration. The Vatican obviously thought it would make a fitting stop for visiting bishops and Cardinals. In 1777, another remodel took place. The current Pope, Pius VI, was scheduled to stop by San Gimignano, and workers once again invaded the palazzo to bring it up to the pope's standard. (In reality, it was the standard of a Cardinal who thought the place dreary and outdated.) The town, in cooperation with the diocese donated a lot of money to make the Palazzo a fitting rest stop for his holiness. Craftsmen went to work straight away, repainting, gilding and beautifying the mansion. The pope's trip however was cancelled, much to the dismay of the devoted parishioners. However, the elegant furnishings and artwork remained, to be enjoyed by future, albeit temporary residents of the Palazzo.

Enzo could hear the siren of opportunity wailing. He managed to study the Conte's face briefly when they last had a conversation, when the Conte first met the boys. It was not a look of slight bemusement that most men have when coming across such youthful charm. It was a look of longing.

A look of hunger.

Enzo had seen that hunger and capitalized on it. A couple of times in his life, at the tavern, he had been approached by men who would offer to buy him a drink. Enzo, never one to refuse free liquor, would always accept. These very men had the same look he saw on Gaspari's countenance. The men he met at the tavern, those men who supplied him with booze only wanted to talk, most of the time. He could always fake friendship; it was merely acting on his part. Still, a few hinted at a chance to take the 'friendship' farther. Enzo always managed to string them along, getting them to pay for another round or two. He didn't care, he had no feelings of guilt at all. They were *'finucchio'*; homosexuals, and they deserved to be swindled. On one occasion though, Enzo had to pay his dues.

It was after a grueling day and Enzo wanted to forget his troubles for a tiny bit. He entered a bar, not the one he normally frequented. This one was conveniently located a few steps from where he was working at the time. There were hardly any patrons since it was just the end of the work day. He ordered, took his glass and sat down. He was disgusted that he only had enough money for one drink. He damned his wife for controlling his money, then he damned those two brats he sired for being the recipient of his hard earned cash. Just then, a man about his age came up to him and started a conversation. The man was pleasant, too pleasant. Enzo knew pretty much what was going to happen next and relaxed. If he played his cards right, he could scam this man for a least two or three rounds. He smiled at the man and used his charm. A few minutes passed but still the man didn't offer. Damn him, Enzo thought! By now, the desire to drink was overwhelming. He dropped a hint about how a man needed some refreshment after a long hard day. Although the man concurred, no offer was forthcoming. He cursed the man silently. Surely no one could be that dense. The craving had turned to severe necessity by then. The man looked at him and asked what was wrong. Enzo put on his sad face. He told the man how hard his life was, how he didn't have any friends, and could he possibly refill his mug? The man smiled and moved closer. In a low voice, he spoke close to Enzo's ear. He didn't mind buying Enzo a drink. In fact, he would even give Enzo some money to get really intoxicated. Enzo was overjoyed. The man said he really would like to, but what was in it for him? Enzo licked his lips, which had gone dry by then. Well? The man asked again. Enzo knew what the man was asking for. He wasn't stupid, merely desperate. The man said that behind the tavern was a small, empty stable. If Enzo wanted some money, he would need to meet him there in a few moments. Then the man stood up and left.

Enzo sat there looking at his empty mug, with absolutely no thoughts except one. He needed that mug filled. He stood and exited the bar. He entered the dark and dank stable and called out "hello." The man said "here, over here." Enzo walked in, fully conscious of what would happen next. Enzo entered the stall. The man pushed him gently to the wall. He kissed Enzo hard on the mouth. Enzo did not kiss back. He got on his knees and began to undo Enzo's trousers. Enzo stood there like a statue, wondering how much money he would be getting.

When the deed was done, he gave Enzo a couple of bills and said that perhaps they might see each other again. Enzo nodded and walked out of the stable, like nothing much had happened. He didn't care, he had money. He could get drunk and put this and everything else behind him.

That was a year ago. Enzo had long since forgotten the whole incident. He wasn't repulsed. To him, it was just a matter of getting paid. Now, he would be doing the same thing, but this time, the stakes were higher. Everyone knew how rich the Conte was. If he played his cards right, he could finally pay off his debts, buy Gabrielle a new dress or even a new house! And he would get his mother one of those new-fangled devices that you peered into, what were they called? His new boss had one. You looked into it and you could see all kinds of places, with depth that gave it such realism. What was it called? A *'Zograscope'*, yes, he would buy his mother a Zograscope.

Enzo walked up the steps of the Palazzo. He was about to raise the knocker when he realized that people of his social standing did not come up to the front door. He didn't want the Conte to think him so insolent or presumptuous, so he went around the back to look for a servant's entrance. He finally found it and knocked. The door was answered by a man in a waist-coat and a white linen shirt. Even the servants are better dressed than I, he thought. He asked for the Conte, and reiterated to the manservant that he was summoned and expected. The man told Enzo to follow him. They made their way through narrow stairs, a long corridor and finally to a vestibule where he was told he could wait. He waited, afraid to sit lest someone else come in to yell at him to get off the furniture. He walked around, studying the portraits that lined the longest wall. None of the people in the portraits were smiling.

Finally, the servant came in again. He told Enzo that the Conte would see him now, and they started walking down another hallway. The servant told Enzo that he should always address the Conte in the proper manner, calling him 'Signor" or better yet "Your lordship." Enzo understood.

The man opened the door and ushered Enzo in. The room was enormous, beautifully paneled in mahogany, lined with hundreds of books from ceiling to floor. The center of the room was dominated by a large mahogany desk. Behind the desk sat Conte Gaspari, reading several documents placed on top of it. Standing next to the Count was a larger man, with a scowl. He was bald and had practically no neck. Enzo would not like this man to be an enemy.

The Conte stopped reading and looked up.

"Ah. Signor Lorenzo Vespucci. I thank you for taking the time to see me!" Gaspari gushed. He signed one more document, all the while talking, and handed that to the muscular man.

"By the way, this is my manservant, Bruno Bragantti. Bruno used to hurt people in the ring. Now, he makes sure that I do not get hurt" he chuckled.

"Signor Bragantti." Enzo nodded at the large man's direction.

"Your lordship, do you need me to stay?" Bruno asked, with a voice so hoarse that it sounded like footsteps on gravel.

"No, no, that will be all. Grazie, Bruno." The servant left the room.

"Thank you for inviting me, your lordship," Enzo answered, remembering the proper form.

"Please sit. Have you had breakfast? Perhaps some tea?" Lorenzo declined politely.

Gaspari began to talk about how the arts were important to the country, no, to the world. How the world needed craftsmen and musicians and other resources of beauty, which was why Lorenzo was here today. Gaspari was a patron of these arts. He felt a need to help the arts and their artists that God only knows were poorly paid. Lorenzo agreed by nodding. Gaspari continued to state that the Renaissance was over, but that didn't mean the proliferation of the arts would stop. No! This country would once again be the great center that it was, possibly greater than what it was during the time of the Medicis!

The Conte, still standing continued to describe the majesty of music and painting. Enzo shifted uncomfortably, patience running thin. Still, it would not do to interrupt the Count, so he kept silent.

Gaspari concluded his monologue, stating that it was a moral imperative that he, as a passionate supporter, felt compelled to call this meeting. He looked at Lorenzo.

"I have traveled to many places, Signor Vespucci, and never have I heard what I heard yesterday. Your boys have the voices of angels."

"Si, Signor Gaspari. I am very lucky." He replied, not once believing what he uttered.

"Luck has nothing to do with it. God has decided in his wisdom to give these boys a special gift. A gift that must be developed to its utmost potential."

"Your lordship is filled with wisdom." Lorenzo ventured, thinking that a little flattery wouldn't hurt.

"Allow me to cultivate that potential. I will take care of all their needs. They will sing for the glory of God."

"Grazie, Signor, molto grazie," Enzo murmured. Then, he added "the offer is more than generous but, ah…"

"But what, my good man?"

"But the boys, they cannot go. I need them, your lordship, to help me in my work. Without them, my income would be awfully affected." Lorenzo whined.

The Conte already knew that Lorenzo would try to milk him. Such insolence! Still, he had to admit that the man was only making good a once in a lifetime chance. He had to give him that.

"I know this, Signor Vespucci. Aside from paying for their needs, I also wish to help your family with a small token to signify our contract."

"The Conte Gaspari is only too kind." Gaspari then proposed a sum that he felt was appropriate.

Lorenzo again praised Gaspari for his benevolence, but stated his mother was sick, his wife was pregnant, and he had debts.

Gaspari played the game. He offered ten percent on top of the original sum proposed.

Again, Lorenzo extolled the munificent virtues of the Count, but his only cow had just died and that he only had one chicken left in the coop.

Gaspari smiled. This man was indeed a rogue. However, it was time to end the charade.

"Signor Vespucci, I will present you with my final proposal. But before you give me your answer, let me tell you something. First, I know for a fact that the boys do not help you in your job. You have been jobless for almost three months. Your debts, as you call them, are the result of your gambling. Your mother may be sick, but your wife is not pregnant, although she has been in bed these past couple of days. As we speak, she is already better, so much so that she is already up and walking. By next week, I am sure she will be once again at her stall where she sells fish. I also know for a fact that you don't even own a cow."

Lorenzo was about to defend himself when Gaspari raised his hand to stop him. Gaspari stared at him intensely.

"I have much influence in your diocese, in your city. You can agree to the price which I think is more money that you will ever see in your lifetime. Or…" he paused, reached for the brocaded velvet strip and pulled on it, "I can make your life so infinitely intolerable for you that you will want to hand the boys over for free. That, Signor Vespucci is my final offer. I will give you a couple of days to discuss this with your wife. You may leave." Gaspari went back to his documents. Lorenzo stood dumbfounded. He realized that anything he said at this point could have repercussions. The door opened and Bruno entered.

"Yes, your lordship?"

"Kindly escort our guest, Bruno"

"Si, Signor Conte," Bruno nodded and looked at Lorenzo.

Lorenzo thought for a few seconds then said in a resigned tone of voice "Thank you very much for seeing me, your lordship."

Gaspari did not even look up from his papers, though inwardly he was satisfied. The boys would come home with him.

Chapter 11

The trip to L'Aquila, the closest town to where Palazzo Gaspari was located, was a long one. The boys sat in the carriage with the Conte who stared at their beatific faces. He'd stare out at the scenery but was compelled to look at them again and again. He studied their features with intense scrutiny, like a jeweler examining a ruby, only to find it flawless. He sighed. He wanted to touch their faces so badly, to caress their porcelain cheeks but kept his hands to himself.

The Count was not a pedophile. He did not wish to touch these boys in a sexual way. He wasn't like that at all. He was sexually drawn to both men and women, but not children. His compulsion was the same with many other people who collected beautiful and fine things. Like any collector, he enjoyed the thought of being able to admire and appreciate the things he possessed. He also loved to handle them. Still, he stopped himself. He did not want to scare the twins. Emanuele could not wait for the boys to start their training. What showpieces they could be at the parties he often threw. He knew his friends would die of envy.

The boys, meanwhile, spoke little. They were already homesick. Vincenzo remembered the day his father came home to announce the Conte's plans for them. Gabriella was still weak, but was feeling better. She had managed to eat a little broth that Annunziata, though still paralyzed, had made. Their father, who never had a good word for them, who beat them even when there was no occasion, suddenly was asking them if they wanted to go on a trip. They looked at him suspiciously.

"It is going to be an adventure!" he exclaimed excitedly.

"Whad drip?" Annunziata asked. Although half her mouth still couldn't move, she managed to communicate well enough.

"Il Conte Gaspari has graciously offered his patronage to the boys. They will stay with him for a while. They will attend the *Colegio*, where they will be trained to become famous opera singers!"

The boys looked at each other. Although a trip did sound adventurous, they didn't want to leave their mother nor their grandmother.

Their mother protested weakly. Annunziata followed suit.

"They don't need to go anywhere. They can remain here, to sing in the choir. When they get older, Father Russo already told me he would train them," Gabriella said.

"Listen!" Lorenzo barked, "This is a rare opportunity!"

That whole day, Enzo did his best to persuade the two women. Annunziata and Gabriella were against the whole endeavor, but Enzo's unrelenting efforts wore them down.

By the end of the day, Enzo had them thinking about their refusal. He finally sat them down and in a pleading voice asked "Don't you want what's best for them?"

Despite their misgivings, both women knew that there were no other options in San Gimignano. Enzo continued to rationalize; the boys would grow up, get married and work menial jobs that would guarantee them a life too close to poverty. Even with Father Russo mentorship, even if their talents did develop in maturity, that was too far in the future. It wasn't sure. This was sure.

He appealed to the spiritual side of Annunziata. He said that God gave them these children a gift, a talent. It was meant to be shared. God didn't want them to sing in a small town choir forever. This was God's will.

To Gabriella, he said that the boys were assured by the Conte that they could come back every year for a visit. (A small lie, but effective.) That '*Il Conte*' was going to help the family's finances with "nominal remuneration," to which he told Gabriella an amount one tenth the real amount he was offered.

The less they knew the better.

Finally, he said that to turn down the offer of the Conte would be impolite, discourteous and would have consequences for him in the community. Think about his reputation! (Which was a laugh, he already had a reputation in town for being a rascal.)

Annunziata prayed about it. Gabriella thought it over. The next morning, with heavy hearts, they told Enzo to thank the Count, and to please look after their boys.

On the day Giaochinno and Vincenzo were supposed to leave, Gabriella packed a small suitcase. Lorenzo was right, she kept telling herself. This was an opportunity of a lifetime. Still, she could not hold back the tears that fell on the garments. Before she closed the bag, she took the only photograph she owned of herself. It was a small photograph. She turned it over and wrote a simple message. She then placed it in a handkerchief she had painstakingly embroidered when she was pregnant with the boys. She stuck it between one of the boys shirts. They would find it eventually. When they did she hoped that they would talk about her, tell each other how they miss her.

Outside, Lorenzo was sitting on his haunches, whittling a piece of wood with his hunting knife. Vincenzo came up to him and asked what he was doing. The question wasn't born out of curiosity. Lorenzo never spoke with the boy except to berate him, and Vincenzo needed something to start the conversation with.

"What do you think I'm doing, stupid?" Vincenzo felt the futility of getting his father to converse, but he pressed on, desperately hoping for his father to say something about their leaving.

"What's it going to be, Papa?"

"Nothing. I'm just whittling wood." Vincenzo stood closer to his father who stood up immediately.

"Bah! You even take the fun out of whittling!" he cried, throwing his knife straight into the ground. He took the piece of wood and hurled it far away. From inside, Annunziata screamed for Lorenzo.

"What does the old biddy want now?" Lorenzo muttered under his breath and went inside. Vincenzo stood there for a while, contemplating the morality of what he was going to do next.

He pulled the knife out of the ground and studied it. It wasn't very large, but in the boy's tiny hands it looked it. Vincenzo ran his thumb along the dark, wooden handle that had a carving of a large 'V'. Making sure that no one was looking, he took the knife and carried it inside. He proceeded to his room, saw the suitcase and decided to place the blade inside that. In his mind, he convinced himself that his father was heartbroken about their departure, and had given him a suitable parting gift.

The boys left the next day. Annunziata and Gabriella

hugged them and kissed them repeatedly.

The boys promised to be good and not to cross their benefactor. Enzo walked them to the Palazzo. Annunziata would not be able to make the trip, and Gabriella was too dispirited to do so.

The Conte was overjoyed at seeing the twins. He handed Enzo the money, to which Enzo thanked him profusely, then he looked at the boys and whispered ominously to them, "Don't embarrass me," he said and left, without even saying goodbye.

The Conte had wanted to spend a little time with them, but had to attend to a few pressing matters first, so he summoned the major-domo, to attend to the children. The major-domo had gotten a maid to attend to the boys. The Conte had already told him to secure some traveling clothes, which he did expeditiously.

When the boys were dressed, the Conte remarked that they looked like little princes. He told them not to be afraid, that they were his guests. They would be leaving soon. It would be a long trip and that they would ride with the Count in his carriage. Also riding with them was the Conte's minder, Bruno, who looked at them malevolently.

They stopped twice that day to change horses and to eat. Suffice to say, they were well fed since they were traveling with the Conte who knew only the better establishments. Then they arrived at Perugia, where they would spend the night at the house of the Count's friend. The boys were escorted to a bed, larger than they've ever seen before. They weren't able to nap during the trip, so now they were totally exhausted. They changed into their sleepwear and fell promptly asleep, dreaming of nothing.

When they arrived at Palazzo di Gaspari, they were

astounded by its sheer size. The edifice was a grand palatial house done in the high renaissance style. It was not the original palazzo, which was a medieval castle located just a few miles south. The 'new' palazzo was built by Emanuele's great-great grandfather who couldn't stand the austere fashion of the castle. With great cost, he built the Palazzo. When it was completed, the family moved in, transforming the old castle into a winery.

The Conte disappeared for a while as the boys stood at the vestibule. Servants rushed in and out with trunks and assorted luggage. Just then, an eighteen year old boy showed up. He was dressed in the fashion of a second footman. He introduced himself as Matteo and told the boys that he was assigned to assist them. With the exception of Bruno, all of the Gaspari staff was pleasant to the eye. This boy could have been mistaken for the twin's older brother. The boys immediately took a liking to Matteo who was extremely easy going and affable. Matteo took them on a tour of the grounds and the castle, showing them where everything was. He also taught them what they had to know while staying at the Palazzo. They were not to disturb the Count. When summoned, they had to be immediately available. Above all: no rough-housing. They could hurt themselves, or worse, be disfigured. Then they would be turned away. The Conte could not tolerate imperfection.

The boys quickly became accustomed to the rhythm of their daily schedule. A teacher was temporarily assigned to them. An older gentleman, a *'professore'* instructed them in all things academic, and a younger one honed their musical skills.

A week later, the Conte threw a party in honor of his

first cousin's birthday. At the end of the dinner, the twins were scheduled to perform. They sang *"Dona Nobis Pacem"* a traditional Latin piece sung in the round, accompanied only by a cellist.

When they finished, the crowd was deathly silent, stunned by the sheer beauty of what they had just heard. Then, the Conte stood and yelled *'bravissimo'* and the assembly exploded in a thunderous applause.

Giaochinno and Vincenzo went on to perform a dozen more times. Once, they sang for a real prince who thought them mystical, and sent them a gift of matching outfits, richly embroidered with sapphires for buttons. Maybe it was because it was their thirteenth performance. Their music teacher had chosen a German lieder. It wasn't a difficult piece, but necessitated long breaths. The crowd was delighted as they launched into the song, but towards the end, tragedy struck. Vincenzo's voice cracked.

Chapter 12

The vocal calamity that occurred was hardly noticeable to those whose ears were not acutely trained. Unfortunately, the Conte's was. The little episode bothered him for a whole fortnight.

The Conte Gaspari could not sing. He spent his money in buying someone else's voice. It was as if it was his voice. He owned it. Now, he was losing it. He found himself returning to the problem every so often. It invaded his conversations, his work, even his sleep. To disregard it, he decided to throw a dinner party for a few of his friends. That might cheer him up. It would be a small event, perhaps just twenty people. He told his secretary to come up with a list of those whom he found most entertaining. Subconsciously he told the secretary to add a few more to the list; a physician who specialized in the throat, a brilliant choirmaster, an illustrious and well-known tenor.

The party arrived promptly, looking forward to the culinary surprises that awaited them, although most of them came to hear the twins perform once more. As expected, the Conte rose to the occasion, plying the appreciative crowd with rich food and fine wine. After the second course, the physician asked if the twins would be singing for them tonight. Damn him! The Conte cursed inwardly. This fete was supposed to make him feel better, and here he was being reminded of the thorn that plagued him. Emanuele answered that they were indisposed. That was when the choirmaster began his lament about the lack of real Italian talent. The tenor said he wasn't aware there was a lack. They all began to take sides as to whether there was or not. The Conte didn't take sides but was curiously listening. The physician agreed with the tenor. Italy could always boast of the best talent. After all, had they not, on occasion, heard the twins perform? The tenor said "Hear, hear!" The choirmaster then presented his query. He said they were truly marvelous, but how old were they now? What happens when they get older?

"So their voices mature with them," The doctor said.

"And no longer maintain the purity we have come to love," the choir master lamented.

The tenor then stated that the purity would be replaced by maturity, and he ran off a list of gifted singers, tenors and baritones who had started as boy sopranos. He himself was one.

They all agreed that the boys would be singers of unparalleled caliber, considering that they had such a good musical foundation.

"Si," the doctor interjected, "upon puberty, the larynx will begin to develop, and their voices will deepen."

"That is, unless they are gored by a wild boar," the tenor added jokingly.

"Then they will be sopranos forever!" The choirmaster ended the punch line. The dinner table erupted in laughter.

The reason for the laughter was simple. The origin for the practice of castration began in a theological paradox. The church had forbidden women to perform in church, or participate in theatre, or in the public stage for that matter. However, by the late 1500's, as music began to be more complex and works for all kinds of entertainment were booming, a mad rush to find men who could play women's roles became apparent. Men could play women's roles, but only a few could sing the more difficult pieces. Since a woman's range was far wider than a man's, the early impersonators were 'falsettist' who used their falsetto register. But still, they didn't sound like real women. Enter the Castrato, or *Castrati*, the plural form.

The Castrati played a fascinating role in the history of singing. Castration had been in existence for centuries as a form of punishment. For the most part, slaves were castrated and then used as harem guards or as servants or tutors for upper class women. The castration process was to make the slaves more docile, less sexual. What was noticeable was that these slaves, castrated at young age, maintained their boyish voices, even when their bodies grew normally.

The voice of the Castrato was phenomenal. The lung capacity and diaphragmatic support was amplified to an astonishing degree. He could sustain the longest notes, projecting tones up to a minute or more, which is beyond the ability of most normal adult male and female singers. The mature castrato was a boy soprano with all the physical resources of a grown man while maintaining the angelic voice of a child.

By the early sixteenth century, a great need for the Castrati arose. Since the deliberate process of mutilation was illegal (despite the Church's employment of eunuchs in their choirs,) all kinds of reasons were used to justify the existence of a particular castrato, such as disease of the testes or accidental injury--being gored by a wild boar was a common reason. It became, sociologically speaking, an inside joke.

The production of castrati almost always took place in Italy. Historically speaking, a significantly large number of castrations during the 18th century had been mentioned. Some state that as many as four thousand each year. Most of these boys came from poor families, from all different parts of the country. Poverty was often provided as the reason for their castration. Parents allowed the operation, hoping for riches and fame that comes from being a great castrato. There would be thousands of boys castrated that would never make it to the elusive top. A very restricted few advanced and would join the great opera houses. The next best, still a small number would enter the best choirs or minor leads. Finally, those of less significant talent would end up as traveling performers or ordinary church choirs. In the late 1700's, one Englishman observed that all the castrati in the churches in Italy were made up of the refuse of opera houses.

The castrato who possessed the finest voice became an operatic idol. By the eighteenth century, *opera seria* had made the Castrato a cultural icon, transformed into popular idols of the time. Like today's rock performers, they too had fame, wealth and status. Regarded as international stars, they could charge enormous, costly fees.

Manzuoli, for example, a popular castrato from Florence, charged 1500 pounds to open the opera season. One must note that the average annual wages for a maid then was six pounds.

Then there was Farinelli. Carlo Broschi, known as Farinelli, had a legendary voice that spanned over three octaves. He had an immense capacity to hold a note for a whole minute without taking a breath. He was unanimously called the Castrato of all Castrati. While performing in London, he was showered with accolades for his vocal agility and uncommon power. Farinelli was invited to all the royal houses. He was invited to sing for Philip V, then king of Spain. His singing was said to have so improved the King's condition, supposedly bouts of mania and depression, that the king asked him to stay to be part of the royal entourage.

Slowly, the popularity of the castrato waned. When Gaspari had discovered the twins, *opera seria* was not as fashionable anymore, since the presence of women in secular performances were beginning to become more common and acceptable. Still, a few purists maintained the clarity of the *Castrati* could rival a woman's any given day.

The dinner party concluded their conversation, only because the ladies in the room would not allow the men to discuss it any longer. The Conte called the servants to bring out dessert and the assembly began to talk about the newest in fashion, the double breasted waist coat. The choral conductor said that if the double breasted waist coat seemed too constricting, he could always get a tailor to let it out.

"Snip, snip," he said, making cutting motions in the air. While fashion talk ruled the table, the Conte Gaspari realized that the boys would soon hit puberty, their voices changing with their bodies. That would not do. He reminded himself to talk to Bruno about it. Bruno knew many people who were willing to do anything for a price. Then, he thanked the choirmaster, who didn't understand why the Conte was doing so. The Conte laughed, telling him that his insight to the world of fashion may have given the Conte a brilliant answer to his predicament.

Chapter 13

The boys had begun to wonder why they had not been summoned for a fortnight now. There had been a dinner party just last week, but they were not asked to perform. This troubled Giaochinno more than Vincenzo. Giaochinno had gotten used to living in the Palazzo, to having everything he needed, to having beautiful clothes and fine food and even having his own servant.

Giaochinno blamed Vincenzo about the singing *faux pas* he had committed. Vincenzo, in turn, claimed that it was accidental. While growing up, they had never really fought over anything. But Giaochinno felt that Vincenzo needed to take his art more seriously. Vincenzo called him stupid. Giaochinno in turn called him a good for nothing. The dispute progressed to a round of fisticuffs. The older boy landed a blow on Vincenzo's face. As they struggled on the floor, the door opened. Luckily, Matteo entered just as Giaochinno was about to land a second blow. Matteo pulled the boys apart then castigated them for such misbehavior. Did he need to tell the Conte? No, they both answered. Matteo asked them if he could trust that this wouldn't happen again. No, they would not fight again. When Matteo left, the whole day passed without Gio and Vincenzo speaking to each other.

Upstairs, in the Conte's opulent salon, Bruno was reporting on the outcome of his master's last instructions. The Conte confided in him a few days back about a task. The Conte needed Bruno to find someone skilled in the surgical arts, who could perform an operation that was obviously illegal.

Someone who could be bought and kept quiet.

Bruno assured his master that he would find the person for the job. Bruno did, for that was what Bruno did well. That-- and breaking bones.

He told the Conte that there was a barber from a nearby village, (barbers at the time were also the village surgeons) who suffered from a series of circumstances that painted him a likely candidate. The barber, a weasel of a man that went by the name of Titino, had been known to have performed this very same surgical procedure on a boy or two. He had debts, a pregnant wife. Most importantly, he had a private habit. Titino was addicted to opium. Bruno, using money and a little persuasion (and Bruno could be very persuasive) convinced the barber of helping him. The barber hesitantly said yes. All that was needed now was a place. Bruno wanted it done away from the Palazzo, so as to keep the good name of his master safe in the unlikely event they were caught. Bruno would claim that he had taken the boys on an outing, where a wild boar had gored them. The Conte laughed.

Bruno also suggested to the Conte the old stable that was located just outside the walls of the medieval castle. It had been abandoned for a long time now. Bruno wanted it done tomorrow, as quickly as possible. The barber might get cold feet. Emanuele agreed, gave Bruno the money he needed and bid him adieu.

The next day, which was a Friday, the boys didn't think it strange that Matteo was noticeably absent after lunch. Their music teacher didn't arrive either at two o'clock, their regular time for lessons. They were told also that the other *professore* was away, so there would be no Latin or German lessons either. They were told to go to their rooms. They had a visitor.

The boys, still somewhat homesick, immediately knew their mother had arrived. They ran down the halls laughing and skipping, much to the annoyance of the servants that they inconvenienced. They got to their room and opened the door. It wasn't their mother. Instead, it was the Conte's personal man-servant, Bruno Bragantti.

Immediately their mood sobered.

Bragantti was standing in the middle of the room, holding a parcel wrapped in brown paper. Bruno told the boys that they were to go with him, and to get ready. Bruno would meet them outside by the small grotto of the Virgin. Did they know where it was? The boys nodded. Good, Bruno said. He then instructed the boys to change into something less fine. As he said this, he threw down the parcel.

Bragantti left wordlessly.

The twins opened the parcel and found some plain linen shirts and rough trousers on the bed. They dressed slowly, all the while speculating as to where they were going. Giaochinno, trying to sound brave, hypothesized that maybe they were going to be put to work. These were after all work-man's clothes. Vincenzo anxiously tried to believe what his brother was telling him. After changing, they walked down the seemingly deserted hall. They exited through a rare used door of the Palazzo, which was the most obvious one to use. It would take them to the path that led to the grotto.

It wasn't a very long walk. When they got to the grotto, they could still see the roof of the Palazzo. Maybe there was a special novena? Giaochinno once again theorized. Vincenzo looked at the Statue of the Virgin that stood on a hollowed out part of a rock wall. He made the sign of the cross, silently asking the Virgin to keep them safe.

Bruno came out from among the bushes. He brusquely told them to follow him.

"Scusi, Signor Bruno..." Giachinno began.

"Silenzio!" Bruno hissed. Obviously, there would be no answers forthcoming. He led them to another clearing, where a small cart drawn by a horse was waiting. The boys clambered up the side of the cart, as Bruno went up front. Pretty soon, the single horse was pulling them at a leisurely pace.

Giaochinno and Vincenzo saw the roof of the Palazzo slowly disappear from view. The sun would now begin its slow descent.

After a while, the boys saw the looming figure of the *Castile*, said to be haunted. Matteo had once told them that the ghosts of a woman killed by her lover still walked its halls, looking for revenge. Giaochinno, ever the adventurer, had always longed for a chance to explore it, maybe find a secret passage that would lead to treasure. Vincenzo however, feared ghosts and told his brother time and again that that it was just an old building, with no mysteries. They had wanted so much to talk now, but thought it best not to. They stopped in front of what looked like a large, low barn. Bruno told them to get out.

"This way," he said. They entered the only entrance. They walked past a few stalls, noticing the sunlight peeking through loose boards. The sun, as if to signal the end of its work, released a last great ray of light that created fingers of brightness that seemed to clutch at them. They walked through the radiance, detecting the dust motes that hung in the air. At the end of the corridor, a runt of a man was washing his hands on a bucket full of water. "They are here."

"You didn't tell me there were two!" the barber whined.

"Shut your whining." Bruno commanded him,

"You will be paid double."

"Did you do as I told you? Did you make them take a long warm bath?"

"There wasn't time." Bruno answered.

Bruno gruffly grabbed Giaochinno and pushed him against a large beam. An old, large iron ring was attached to the beam. In one quick motion Bruno picked up a piece of rope lying on the foot of the beam and began to tie the boy's hands. Giaochinno was at first too dumbfounded to say or do anything. When he found his hands tied though, he began to struggle but Bruno was obviously too strong. Vincenzo ran to his brother, but Titino grabbed him. As Vincenzo tried to escape, Bruno slipped the rope across the ring, raising Giaochinno's arms up high. He secured the line. Vincenzo was sobbing uncontrollably by now, while Giaochinno was screaming at Titino to let go of his brother. The large man then took Vincenzo and slammed him down of the platform of an inclined, upturned cart. He began to tie Vincenzo's right arm to a wheel.

"Signor Bruno, please--" Vincenzo sobbed as his left arm was secured also.

"Signor Bruno, I promise I will sing better, better than Giaochinno, better than anyone, please--" Then Bruno smiled. He was enjoying this. He grabbed the lapels of the boy's thin shirt and yanked hard. A ripping sound reverberated like nails on a slate. Bruno then began to undo the boy's pants.

"No!" yelled Giachinno. His eyes had grown wide with fear. He had heard stories like this. He honestly thought Bragantti would rape Vincenzo. "Don't you dare touch him! Bastard! Son of a whore!" Invectives streamed out of Giaochinno's mouth, words like pebbles hurled ineffectually at armor. Bruno turned his face to look at him. He then grabbed a rag and approached Giaochinno. He stuffed the rag in the boy's mouth, making him gag.

"Don't worry, you'll be next." He patted the boy's cheek almost lovingly.

He returned to Vincenzo, who was by now reduced to whimpering in fear. Bruno yanked the boy's trousers off, leaving the boy splayed naked as when he was born. His legs were tied then also.

Giaochinno tried to scream, but the rag was highly effective.

"Will you use the opium?" Bruno asked Titino.

"No. I have used it before, but I observed that most of those who had been cut after this manner died by the Narcotick. I think it more advisable to practice a better method." Truth be told, Titino had used the last of the opium a couple of days ago. The same opium he was supposed to use on the boys.

"What would that be?" Bruno asked.

"You simply press the jugular, this will make the boy stupid and insensible."

"He would fall into a kind of apoplexy--" Bruno remarked.

"The operation could be performed with nary any pain at all to the patient," Titino ended. Titino had done it this way twice already. He was confident that it would work well.

Bruno put his large hands on the neck of the boy. Vincenzo said 'please' one last time before Bruno began to apply pressure. When the boy's body turned limp, Titino took out a long knife. Giaochinno's eyes widened.

Cupping Vincenzo's scrotal sac, the barber began to work the knife slowly in a sawing motion.

Intermezzo

"Signor Vespucci?" Bennett called the man's name softly. Vespucci had been talking for nearly an hour. He grew suddenly silent after recounting the painful ordeal.

"Would you like to continue tomorrow?"

When no answer was forthcoming, Bennett stood up.

"I am so sorry that you had to go through that," the young doctor said apologetically. He felt that needed to say something more, but couldn't think of anything else. Bennett needed to be let out and was about to rap on the door when he heard Vespucci whimper.

"Why?" the old man asked softly.

Bennett was unsure of how to answer the question. "I cannot tell you why, Signor."

"Vincenzo and I were taken to the *Colegio.* For six years, we spent learning all there was to learn about music. Our voices were our instruments, and we practiced those instruments day in and day out. I did well, but Vincenzo…"

"Yes?" Bennett prodded.

"Vincenzo was a gifted student, but a lazy one. He constantly kept to himself. He didn't try to make friends with any of the students, preferring instead to stay in his room. A room we shared, by the way."

"So you completed your training and then…"

"When I had completed my training, I was quickly offered a lead role in Milan. It was Handel's Xerxes. I think that it was mostly due to Conte Gaspari's connections. He was a good patron. Then, a few years later, I found myself in Florence performing the same role. It was 1829…"

Chapter 14

In the fall of 1829, the constant mood of anxiety that blanketed the northern part of Italy began to lift. The reason for all this concern began with a small pox epidemic which had begun a few years back in Liguria. Widespread vaccinations were ordered, which was first introduced by the French, when Napoleon had invaded that part of Italy a decade ago.

In Florence, rumors of the outbreak punctuated by stories of death began to die down. Still, Florentines would only hire servants and nurses who were pockmarked. Their scars a sure sign that they had battled the illness and won. One such young woman, Serpina Egitto, was one of those survivors. Serpina had contracted the malady when she was 16. A beautiful and intelligent girl, her face was still slightly blemished by scars. Although they began to clear, the most prominent of them would remain visible for the rest of her life. It was on her forehead, a half-moon scar which she would be forever conscious about.

She left Liguria an orphan. The ailment had claimed her entire family, mother, father and little sister. She chose Florence simply because her only living relative, the sister of her father, lived there. It took her a very long time to reach Florence. Thankfully, her aunt took her in. The old lady was working for *La Donna* (the Lady) Abriana Salvi di Tursi, daughter of the Marchese di Tursi. Because of this, she was able to find Serpina employment at the Palazzo di Tursi, on Via de Serragli, a stone's throw from the Piazza Santo Spiritu, current residence of said Donna.

At the age of 17, she began work at the Palazzo di Tursi as a scullery maid, scrubbing pots and pans all day long. Her bright disposition, lack of complaint and hard work was not lost on the housekeeper. After a year, the housekeeper assigned her a new position, that of a lower housemaid. She would have remained in that position, given the large number of women seeking employment, if not for the dog.

The mistress owned a small lap dog, a Spaniel, whom she was very fond of. The dog, for whatever reason had stopped eating. For days, it lay near death, and the mistress was inconsolable. Serpina too, was very much affected. She was very fond of animals ever since she was a child. Seeing the poor dog lying like that was too much for her to bear. One day, when she knew that La Donna was out and all the servants were busy, she went upstairs. She took with her a small morsel, which she had saved from the previous night's dinner. She knew that if she were caught, she would be immediately terminated. However, she would only be in the room for a few minutes. She entered the room cautiously and saw the poor canine lying on his bed, a small cushion. She picked it up and cuddled it, telling it to be well.

Unluckily, the mistress had forgotten something and decided to go back. When the door opened, she spied Serpina, on her knees, talking to an animated creature that for days showed no sign of life. The mistress was overjoyed. She told Serpina that from now on, she would be in charge of the little spaniel. A few months later, when La Donna Abriana's personal maid fell ill, Serpina was a natural choice to take her place, albeit temporarily. She proved to be a perfect substitute. The lady's maid's condition grew from bad to worse. Finally, she died, and Serpina had been La Donna's maid ever since. She was twenty.

As a Lady's Maid, she had to attend to her mistress' needs and appearance. It was very hard work, making sure that the mistress was always looking her best, never needing anything, having the foresight to know what would be required next. In a typical day, she rose at dawn, bringing up tea before breakfast. She then prepared the clothes, which in itself was a task. Since the mistress had to put on so many layers of clothing, she was needed to assist in taking off her first attire, help put on the next. On any given day, the lady had to change costumes at least three times. The wardrobe alone was overwhelming. There was the morning dress, to lounge about the bedroom. Before coming down, the mistress would change into a day dress. If her mistress had scheduled a walk outside, then another change was necessary and a promenade dress would be worn. Before dinner an evening dress. Traveling meant a Carriage dress, a long affair, buttoning close down the front, from the throat to the shoe. There was also the mourning dress, the working dress, the formal gowns.

Aside from that, Serpina also had to facilitate all other matters, such as putting away her jewels, keeping her wardrobe in repair and washing the lace and fine linens, too.

When La Donna woke up, Serpina would attend to her mistress' toilet, arranging her hair and finally dressing her. She would also put out whatever necessities were needed for walking, riding or traveling. She was expected to carry anything the lady needed to take along; parcels, packages, purchases, parasols and petty cash. She sometimes attended the tea service for her lady, with the other housemaids (the front housemaids). Rarely was she called to help serve at the table. Her being there was only a ritual, to serve her lady and female guests. There was enough help in the Palazzo di Tursi, but she still had to be there, lest her lady need something.

She had been on the staff of the di Tursi household for four years when she heard about Giaochinno Vespucci. La Donna Abriana went to the opera with Martina Colon, her best friend and confidant, and an aunt. Serpina was given a rare night off. When the ladies returned, they were all speaking of this Vespucci, a marvelous man who sang like an angel. Clearly, the ladies were excited. Abriana went on and on about his manners, his rumored dalliances, his unconventional behavior. Martina went on about his costumes. Serpina was so wrapped up in their conversation that for a moment, she believed that she too was at the opera. The ladies had said goodnight to each other and Serpina followed Abriana to the bedroom, to lend a hand with the nightly routine. La Donna told Serpina that she had to invite this man to sing at their next affair, wouldn't that be grand?

"Si, Donna Abriana, that would be very good indeed," she replied enthusiastically.

Maybe, just maybe, Serpina would get to meet this man, this icon, this god.

Chapter 15

Vespucci did attend La Donna Abriana's grand affair. In fact, Vespucci became a regular visitor. The staff began to talk amongst themselves about how smitten *la donna* Abriana was. Whenever Vespucci came to visit, Abriana was hopelessly in a tizzy. Everything had to be in place, everything had to be perfect. She herself fretted over what to wear, what to serve, what activities to be scheduled as to amuse the singer but not to tire him too much. Vespucci at the time lived in Venice, but his visits to Florence became more and more frequent. Each time he corresponded with Abriana, she convinced him to stay at the Palazzo di Tursi as her guest, to which he accepted. He stayed on and off the Palazzo for almost half a year.

Serpina did meet Vespucci, as well. Not in the truest sense in the word. She was in attendance the many times that Abriana and him and her other friends got together for tea or some parlor pursuits. They were never introduced, (servants were not introduced to guests.) Still, she believed that he noticed her. She even thought she had caught him staring at her, once, but when she turned to look, he was already engaged in conversation with someone. Whenever she had a chance, she would surreptitiously study him. A very elegant fellow, rather tall but not gangly. He was very well proportioned, and although there was a maturity about him, his face was quite young. He was possibly 24 or 25 years old, with such a smooth complexion. So smooth that the first time she saw him, her hand immediately went up to her forehead, to feel her old scar. He was always dressed elegantly, and always acted confidently. He had an easy going way about him, the way he told stories, the way he laughed, never constrained, but full with so much abandon that it was infectious. He was also a very compassionate man and caring man. He worried constantly about his mother, who was old and lived in San Gimignano. He also voiced concern for his younger twin brother Vincenzo, who he said hated Florence. Vincenzo lived with him in his house in Venice. Once, he recalled the time that he nearly gave Vincenzo a black eye, and they all laughed at the way he told the story.

She noticed that he had an intensity and passion about him that people naturally gravitated towards.

"Signor Vespucci, what do you think? Signor Vespucci, in your estimation--?" It seemed that his opinion was esteemed and much sought after.

When he left Palazzo, it seemed all joy left with him. La Donna was melancholic, the servants were more anxious. Even Serpina herself would find herself sighing, waiting for any word about his next visit.

La Donna would summon Martina to come stay with her, which Martina would do. They went out to the shows and the parties. Martina introduced Abriana to many eligible men, but she complained that none possessed the character and impeccable manners of Vespucci.

When Vespucci did return a month later, it was for to ask the Marchese di Tursi for his daughter's hand in marriage. La Donna Abriana already knew a proposal was imminent, but she claimed it was too soon. She stated this repeatedly to everyone she knew, although deep down she was relieved. (The catastrophe of being unmarried and old was a fate worse than death to any woman of social standing, she thought, and she was already twenty two years old.) No wedding date was fixed, but many thought it to occur by the following year.

One other reason for his return to Florence was to perform a new work, an oratorio, written specifically for him by Jacobo L'Abbate, an up and coming composer. A preview of the oratorio would be staged right in the grand ballroom of the Palazzo di Tursi. It would be the event of the season, with many of Florence's most wealthy and most influential persons invited to pledge support and money to Jacobo's favorite charity: *L'ospedale di Bonifazio.*

It would be a masked ball. The ladies that made up the *crème de la crème* of Florentine society anxiously awaited their invitations from La Donna Claudia di Tursi, wife of La Marchese, mother of Abriana.

Meanwhile, seamstresses, corset makers, wig makers and cobblers all over Florence found themselves swamped with orders for gowns, corsets, wigs and shoes. The unfortunate few, those tardy ladies who took their time to requisition the essential costumes and their accoutrements found themselves turned away by the better craftsmen. Martina, scatterbrain that she was, had to offer more money, up to double than usual, to have her order taken. No one took her up on the offer. She had to travel to Siena, to another city to find a dressmaker who would accommodate her.

No one, absolutely not one of the ladies would dare to wear something that they had worn before, particularly for such a special occasion. They would be the subject of malicious talk, and the focus of much ridicule.

A week before the masked ball, Vespucci arrived at the Palazzo looking tired and weary. He had arrived from London, where his last performance was hailed by critics and theatre-goers alike to be magnificent. A special luncheon would be served in honor of Giaochinno's return to Florence. Abriana was thrilled to see him. She and a few of her friends were on hand to greet him. Vespucci however, seemed pre-occupied and was less eager than her. They proceeded to the great dining room. When they were all seated, the servants began to serve.

Everyone began to talk about this and that. Conversation finally turned to Vespucci's astonishing performance in London.

"Where you there, Signora?" Vespucci asked the lady who presented that fact.

"Ah, no, Signor Vespucci. But I read about it." The lady blushed.

"I see," Vespucci raised an eyebrow contemptuously.

Abriana interrupted, saying that everyone thought he was brilliant, the paper just confirmed it.

After lunch, they retired to the sunroom. There, a woman who was a much sought after fortune teller would read their palms and tell their future. The seer asked who would be first. Abriana declared the Vespucci should be. The other guests were only too happy to let him go first.

The fortune teller asked him to shuffle the cards. Vespucci complied. The psychic looked at the cards and knew something was wrong.

She asked for forgiveness, the cards needed to be shuffled once more. Once again the tarot revealed something far too ominous for the clairvoyant to share with the gentleman. Instead, she gave him a generic pronouncement of meeting a stranger, going on a trip and happiness everlasting. She had wanted to warn him desperately, she knew it deep in her bones, but she couldn't. Her reputation was at stake and she lived off the referrals of wealthy people who invited her for amusement. She prayed a simple prayer instead and asked who would be next.

Giaochinno begged Abriana and her company's leave, stating that the trip was tiring and that he needed to rest. The rest of the group protested his leaving but also murmured their understanding. He left as the fortune-teller read the cards, uttered another prophecy to one of the female guests who screamed with delight.

When he got to his room, one of the footmen assigned to him was in the room, waiting to help him undress. Vespucci climbed into the bed and slept. When he awoke, he felt strange. It was late afternoon outside. The balcony doors, which he kept wide open, let in a cool breeze. The room wasn't dark yet but still Giaochinno lit the candle by the nightstand. He stood up and walked across the room to the vanity. He pulled up the small, low-backed chair and sat. He looked at the mirror on the vanity to study his face. His face seemed to have aged. No, he wasn't staring at his face. His face didn't possess four eyes. It was not his face, and yet, at the same time it was. Someone else was behind him.

"Vincenzo!" he cried.

"Are you glad to see me, brother?" Vincenzo asked.

"Why did you leave me like that?" Giaochinno pouted. Vincenzo merely shrugged.

"I thought you said you would stay in London, that you hated Florence."

"I decided I love you more than I hate Florence." Vincenzo raised his hands to signify his resignation.

"Anyway, I hate it when you disappear to God knows

where," Vespucci said sullenly, almost childlike.

"Ah, but you know I would never abandon you. I promised you that since we were little. You know I keep my promises."

"I don't know, Vincenzo, people always say things they don't mean. Just because you're my brother doesn't mean you're exempt from the human condition."

Vincenzo laughed, which made Giaochinno laugh with him. When his brother was around, things were more bearable.

"Anyway, I'm glad you showed up."

"Why? Tell me..."

"Because you were right. No one here likes me. Everyone here pretends to like me, just like you said in London."

"Aren't you sick and tired of the hypocrisy? Don't you wish you could just end it all?" Vincenzo stared out the window.

There was a knock on the door.

'Enter!'

The door opened and Serpina came in.

"Scusi, Signor Vespucci." She looked around the room as if searching for something.

"And you are?"

"Serpina, Signor Vespucci, Serpina Egitto, La Donna Abriana's maid." She performed a slight curtsy. Vespucci smiled. There was something about this Serpina that reminded him of someone, but he couldn't quite place it.

"Serpina! Serpina, Vincenzo, just like the Serpina in Pergolesi's opera." He looked at Vincenzo who was smiling, lips pressed together, as if to stifle a laugh.

"She was a maid too, you know," he heard Vincenzo

remark to the girl who looked confused. "I'm sorry, Signor, I don't understand."

"What opera was that, Gio?" Vincenzo asked

"Let me see. Ah! 'La Serva Padrona!' She was a very funny character."

Serpina nodded, "And she was a maid," she added.

"Yes!" Vespucci clapped his hands.

"Now, tell me, what is the beautiful Serpina doing in a gentleman's quarters?" Serpina looked down.

"He is only joking." Vincenzo said, "Giaochinno always likes to joke around."

Serpina looked up and said "La Donna said that the musicians are arriving. She told me to tell your valet, but he is missing."

"Just like Vincenzo, always missing." He looked at Vincenzo who was adjusting his sleeves. He looked at Serpina again. "One moment he is here and the next he is gone," Giaochinno said, as Vincenzo grinned. "So you came instead to tell me. That was very considerate of you, Serpina. God knows how musicians hate it when you make them wait. I will be down eventually. If we are lucky, maybe Vincenzo will join us."

"Si, Signor. I will tell them." Serpina begged his leave and left the room.

"She likes you, you know."

"Vincenzo, you really must stop this. Every time I meet a girl you begin to find fault with her." "Can I help it if you always get the prettiest one, while I have no one," Vincenzo said in mock pity.

"Stop it, Vincenzo, just stop it."

"Stop what? You deserve everything you have.

You were always the favorite one."

"That is not true! Why do we always have this conversation?"

"I am sorry," Vincenzo said as he sat on the bed.

"You can be so difficult sometimes."

"All the time, not just sometime." Vincenzo laid down on the bed, raising his arms and putting his hands behind his head.

"Well, I better get dressed." He looked at Vincenzo.

"Aren't you coming?"

Vincenzo yawned in an exaggerated manner. "Suit yourself." Giaochinno said.

***

"Is that a good tempo for you, Signor Vespucci?" the conductor asked. Jacobo L'Abbate was eager to please Giaochinno, seeing how this man could easily make or break his career.

"On measure 89?" Immediately, pages began to turn. "If we can have more legato?" Giaochinno suggested. Pencils came out and the musicians began to write on their scores. The conductor then barked "Measure 89, poco legato." Jacobo L'Abbate may have been the composer of this work and the conductor of this orchestra, but he knew that Giaochinno Vespucci could make or break his career and any suggestions from him were to be treated as law. Was there anything else they needed to go over?

Giaochinno noticed Vincenzo enter. He approached the orchestra and stood next to Giaochinno.

"Signor Vespucci?" Jacobo asked again.

"Forte--measure 68," Vincenzo ordered.

"Anything else?" Jacobo asked Giaochinno again, unmoving, pencil still poised in the air.

"You heard him, Maestro, forte in measure 68."

"Forte, beginning measure 68." Jacobo barked once more and pages turned yet again.

"You wouldn't know a forte if it bit you." Vincenzo said, and left.

"I'm sorry. I see now." Jacobo looked at the score. "That was actually an omission, most probably by the scorer. I could have sworn I put a mark there."

"That's quite all right, Maestro. It is an astounding work. You should be proud." Giaochinno said.

"It is only as astounding as the musicians who give it life."

"You are too kind. *Grazie, Maestro.*"

"Prego, Signor," Jacobo murmured.

Vespucci made his way to where Vincenzo had found a seat. Jacobo began to give last minute instructions as the musicians packed their instruments.

"He hates me," Vincenzo complained.

"He doesn't hate you."

"He's a sniveling, ass-kissing fool," Vincenzo continued.

"If *you* would stop being such an ass, maybe he would like you more."

"And another thing, you think he values your opinions? Your suggestions? He thinks you're a freak."

Giaochinno looked at Jacobo who was speaking to the first violinist. Jacobo looked up and noticed Giaochinno staring at him. He gave him a wave of a hand.

"I think you're wrong, Vincenzo." Giaochinno said, although the way the violinist and composer were talking, he wasn't so sure.

"They're talking about you right now."

"They're going over last minute instructions,"

Giachinno said in their defense.

"Fine. Don't believe your brother. I, who have never lied to you." Vincenzo stood up and was about to exit when the conductor approached Giaochinno.

"Maestro, can you please help." Giaochinno called to Jacobo. Vincenzo looked at Jacobo with contempt.

"We need your help," Giaochinno asked once again. Jacobo looked perplexed.

"I want you to apologize." Vincenzo demanded.

"I'm sorry?" Jacobo asked.

"See…there! Va bene!" Giaochinno cried out.

"Thank you, maestro."

"I still think he's an ass." Vincenzo said as he left.

"I don't understand," the conductor mumbled.

"It's alright. It's difficult sometimes. Even I don't understand." Giaochinno confessed. The maestro scratched his head.

"So, this is our last rehearsal, no?" Giaochinno continued, trying to sound unaffected.

"One more, Signor, but with the choir. You don't need to be there. They are having a difficulty with some of the complicated passages, so I offered to help them with it."

"That is very good of you, Maestro. So many believe that you can achieve music without work, without passion. How little do these people know."

The composer nodded. He knew what Vespucci was talking about. Music without passion was merely sound. Anyone could make sound. To make real music, you needed a soul.

Chapter 16

The next day, Vespucci and Abriana decided to go for a walk along Via San de Serragli. Serpina went with them, since at all times an unmarried lady did not go anywhere with a man unchaperoned. She took the dog, which was in dire need of fresh air.

"How did the rehearsal go?" Abriana asked.

"Very well, thank you. Although we had some difficulty with one passage. We had to repeat it over and over. Maestro Jacobo was very patient though.

He is a very thorough man."

"Oh yes. I think they will offer him a permanent position at the Conservatory."

"He deserves it. He is also very humble."

"Why do say that, Gio?" Abriana asked, using her nickname for him.

"Last night, Vincenzo and he nearly had an argument."

"Your brother was here?" Abriana asked, surprised.

"Yes. Anyway, Vincenzo demanded an apology which the maestro gave."

"So, where is he?" Abriana asked, rather miffed. A gentleman did not come to the Palazzo without presenting himself to the lady of the house. She thought Vincenzo discourteous, but did not say anything to Gio.

"Who knows? Vincenzo comes and goes when he pleases."

Giaochinno looked at her, with a look of resignation. The dog barked unexpectedly. Dottore Enrico Tebaldi came to them. Serpina shushed the canine.

"Ah! Signor Vespucci! La Donna Abriana! How nice

to see you again. Mrs. Tebaldi is so excited about the ball! That is all she ever talks about. That, and hearing the magnificent Signor Vespucci sing." "It is nice to see you again Dottore Tebaldi," Giaochinno said, remembering the man from the last time he was in Florence. Giaochinno had complained to Abriana about a cough he had that didn't seem to get better. Dottore Tebaldi, who had dropped by for tea that day, suggested myrrh, a few drops placed at the very back of the tongue. Vespucci was skeptical but went ahead and tried it. His cough disappeared. Since then, he was grateful to the man. Tebaldi was a medical doctor by profession. Talk was that he belonged to old wealth, and didn't even need to work at all. He was always smiling, always pleasant. He loved music and cigars. He was never seen without one.

They continued walking, talking about unimportant things. The Doctor wished them good health and crossed the street.

"He is such a wonderful man, that Dottore," Abriana announced. They walked back, so that they would be in time for tea.

When tea was over, Abriana excused herself, stating the sun had given her a headache. She kissed Giaochinno briefly on the cheek.

"My beautiful Gio," she said stroking his cheek lightly.

"Abriana", he placed his hand over hers, holding it gently. He brought her hand close to his lips.

"Serpina," she began, "might come in."

"So?" Giaochinno said, still kissing her hands.

"Gio!" Abriana giggled, trying to stop him as his lips moved up her arm. She pulled herself away gently.

"I do need to go. My head is pounding and a little rest will do me well."

"Please stay."

"I cannot."

"Please?" he looked at her with his best impression of a lost puppy. Abriana laughed lightly. "You can be so difficult."

"Just like my brother," Gio smirked.

Abriana looked quizzically at Giaochinno. "You did say he left London and was here in Florence."

"Yes," Gio replied, "I was telling you earlier."

"When did he arrive?"

"A few days ago." He embraced her from behind and started kissing her neck. "I would love for you to meet him."

She turned to him. "If he is anything like you, then I might fall in love with him too. Then what would happen? I would have to choose."

"No, you wouldn't have to. You would be marrying us both." He laughed. Abriana disengaged herself from Giaochinno.

"Well, I do hope he somehow makes it to the ball. I will have an invitation left with you."

"Oh, he'll be there, I promise you," Giaochinno said.

"I really must go. When Serpina comes back, tell her I need her, please Gio?"

Giaochinno nodded. Serpina had left with the other servants to clear the tea service.

Abriana left the room, leaving Giaochinno by himself. Vespucci decided to take a walk in the garden. He looked out the large French doors that led to a small veranda. The outside looked so inviting, a slight wind making the sheer curtains beneath the drapes billow. As he gazed outside, Giachinno was at once surprised to see Vincenzo standing there, looking annoyed and leaning on the low wall. He passed the opened doors, stepping out into the veranda. He leaned on the low wall also.

"You missed tea. More importantly, you missed meeting Abriana."

"La Donna and I will soon meet," Gio heard Vincenzo say it without concern.

"She is looking forward to meeting you."

"I really don't know why you want to marry her. She has a reputation, you know."

"Why, Vincenzo? Why do you say things to hurt me?" This last statement upset Giaochinno visibly.

"I'm merely repeating what I've heard. She doesn't love you. She's using you."

"Using me? For what? She can have any man. Someone far richer than I."

"The Vespucci name is what's she's after."

"Ha! Like the di Tursi name wasn't grand enough!"

"Fine. Be like that."

"Like what?" Gio asked, exasperated.

"Never listening to me. Always choosing others over me."

Choosing. That seemed to be all the Vincenzo ever talked about. He decided to change the subject.

"Anyway, will you be at the ball?"

"Maybe, maybe not."

Giaochinno wanted to ask Vincenzo what he meant, but chose rather to keep silent. He studied his brother's face, trying to get him to speak.

"Ah, here is your lady's maid. Doesn't she remind you

of someone?"

Giaochinno turned to look at the girl who came out of the opened French Doors.

Vincenzo pulled himself up, standing straighter.

"Well, what is it that you want, girl?" Vincenzo asked rudely. Giaochinno felt embarrassed at the tone his brother had used on the frail looking maid. "Scusi, Signor Vespucci. I was looking for La Donna Abriana."

"Ah, she does not feel well, and retired to her bedroom."

"She has a bloody headache--" Vincenzo spat. Once again, Giaochinno felt embarrassed at Vincenzo's incivility.

"Grazie, Signor." She nodded and gave another curtsy.

"Miss Serpina, you don't need to curtsy," Giaochinno said.

"Yes, Serpina, he's not royalty you know," he heard Vincenzo say.

Si, Signor," she nodded.

"I guess you should check on La Donna Abriana to see if she needs anything." Giaochinno suggested.

"Si, Signor," she nodded again, and smiled weakly. She did not move.

Giaochinno was about to say something. He heard Vincenzo interject, rather rudely; "Well? What are you standing there for, girl? Leave us!"

"If I have your leave." Serpina said quietly.

"Of course," Giaochinno smiled back. "I will see you around then," he added. Serpina exited the same way she came in.

"There's another one who wants to get in your pants!"

Vincenzo roared.

"Vincenzo, must you be so vulgar?"

"I'm not vulgar. It's being honest. Anyway, you're just ashamed."

"Ashamed of what?"

"You," Vincenzo said maliciously, "being a freak."

Gio's eyes widened. Not once did he and Vincenzo have a conversation about what happened to them when they were young.

"When she gets in your pants," Vincenzo continued cruelly, "she'll find a couple of things missing."

"Vincenzo!" Giaochinno was shocked.

"I mean, it still works, doesn't it? I know you've touched yourself more than once." Vincenzo's laughter rang in his ears. The laughter went on for a long time. Giaochinno finally decided to go back in. He could still hear Vincenzo's laughter, all the way to the end of the hall.

Chapter 17

Abriana noticed that the last few days, Gio was sullen and not his usual self. She asked him repeatedly if he was fine, but he merely said that nothing was the matter. She attributed it to nerves. Surely even the greatest performers suffered some anxiety before a performance.

The day before the ball, Abriana passed his room. She was about to knock when she heard him shouting. It sounded like an argument, although she couldn't make out the words. She thought of peering into the keyhole. She was very tempted but she stopped herself, thinking about how inappropriate it would be. She was caught between eavesdropping or not, when she heard footsteps coming her way. One of the servants would catch her in the act, and that just wouldn't do.

In the bedroom, Giachinno was distressed, close to tears. He was not one who cried easy, but whenever Vincenzo was involved, he found himself susceptible to crying like a little boy. He had just woken up half an hour ago when he saw Vincenzo sitting in the chair by the window. Vincenzo was staring at him.

"I made love to your wench last night. That little maid, Serpina."

"Vincenzo, it's too early."

"She screamed as I entered her. She clawed my back as I pounded her."

"Vincenzo, I really don't want to hear about your sexual exploits." He stood up and walked to the washstand and splashed water on his face. He toweled his face dry.

"Why not, aren't you the least bit curious about my

manhood?" Vincenzo asked.

Giaochinno ignored him. Vincenzo offensively grabbed his crotch. "Come on, Giaochinno. Here, feel it. I know you want to."

"I need to get dressed, Vincenzo."

"You know, she thought I couldn't perform. She heard that our kind was impotent."

"She heard?"

"This isn't news to you, brother! Everyone tells you how talented you are, but when your back is turned they talk about you."

"That is not true."

"That *is* true. They all laugh about the half man. The man without a prick!"

"They don't say that!"

"She said it, yesterday. I heard her talking with your precious Lady. They were talking about how small your manhood must be."

"La Donna would never--"

"So I fucked her. I did it to punish her."

"Punish her? Punish her?"

"She helped," Vincenzo whispered.

"Helped with spreading a stupid, petty rumor?" Giaochinno snarled.

"You know why!" Vincenzo spat the words out, each word glistening with venom. "You are such a faggot!"

"I need to go get dressed. La Donna is expecting me for breakfast." Giaochinno began to undress.

Vincenzo then began to call his brother other names. Giaochinno told him to leave.

When he found himself all alone in the room, he wept. He wept because Vincenzo was so mean to him. He wept because he loved Vincenzo so much it hurt him. He wept because he was alone again.

Abriana began to grow impatient at the table. She finally told Serpina to have Signor Vespucci's valet summon him. Serpina was about to leave just as Giaochinno arrived.

"I was about to have you called."

"I didn't sleep well. When I woke up, Vincenzo and I had a…discussion. I'm sorry." "Well?" Abriana asked impatiently.

"Well, what, my love?" Gio contested.

Abriana was about to comment on his brother's rudeness, his lack of protocol and etiquette but decided against it. One didn't enter or leave without being announced. She would take the matter up with Lorenzo. No need to upset Gio.

"Isn't he joining us for breakfast, seeing that he's here in the Palazzo?"

"No," Vespucci sighed. "He had to leave."

"So what were you two arguing about?"

"I didn't say argue, Abriana. I said discussion." "My mistake."

"Why would you say that it was an argument?"

"Nothing, really. You looked upset when you walked in. I thought that maybe you and Vincenzo had a fight, as brothers are ought to do."

Serpina approached the table, carrying a small cup. She placed it next to her ladyship.

Vespucci studied her. He looked once again at her features, but her gaze remained at the task at hand. Meanwhile, Abriana was now telling a tale of her cousins, brothers, who would get into fisticuffs even up until now when they were adults.

Giaochinno continued to watch Serpina. He cleared his throat, trying to catch her attention. Serpina looked up, almost alarmed. Giaochinno couldn't tell by her reaction if it was one of guilt or innocence.

"You didn't hear a word I said," La Donna accused him.

"I surely did. Your cousins, having fisticuffs."

"Anyway, they always made up in the end. I'm sure you and Vincenzo will too."

They ate in silence. Giaochinno was afraid that his terseness would produce more uncomfortable questioning about what he and Vincenzo talked about. He cleared his throat again. Abriana looked up.

"Have you fitted your gown yet?" he asked sweetly. Abriana, fashion conscious woman that she was, provided him with more information than necessary about her dress. She also complained that several of the buttons had fallen off when she was fitting it the previous night. She would definitely complain about the shoddy workmanship.

"Serpina did a good job last night though. She spent almost all night redoing them."

"She spent all night redoing them?" Vespucci asked almost eagerly.

"That's what I said," Abriana remarked. "I really mustn't abuse her like that."

"Serpina spent all night redoing your buttons?" he began to laugh. Vincenzo wasn't with her! She was up all night! Redoing buttons.

"What's so funny, Gio?" Abriana could not see the humor in what she had just said.

"Serpina," Vespucci called to her.

"Si, Signor."

"You have made my La Donna happy." He held Abriana's hand. "I daresay that you must be recompensed."

Abriana laughed at Giaochinno's gallantry. Was that why he laughed? Because she was happy with her dress?

"Well, Serpina. I take it you have made our Signor Vespucci pleased as well. What do you say?"

"Signor, no. I mean, *grazie.* I am happy to do it for La Donna. She is very kind to me. You do not need to thank me."

"I do. If your mistress permits, I would like you to hear me sing."

Abriana was slightly surprised to hear her fiancé invite a servant. It was unheard of. Still, it made him so happy, a welcome change from his past sullen mood that it didn't bother her a bit. Serpina deserved it too, she thought. In a cavalier tone, she announced;

"Serpina, Signor Vespucci and I would be very pleased if you were there, if only for the preview of the oratorio."

Serpina's eyes grew wide in disbelief.

"I think I may have something suitable for you to wear even," Abriana continued. "Do you know that blue gown that had a small tear on the right sleeve? You may use that. It is a small tear, you could fix it in a moment. I doubt if I'll ever wear that again anyway."

Serpina stood immobile, trying to understand what was happening. Something like this was tantamount to winning the lottery. Lady's maids were not invited to balls. They were not invited to anything. If they did attend some small function, like tea, they were fixtures, not guests. She nodded, trying not to cry, saying *grazie* to her mistress and her gentleman, repeatedly.

"You are more than welcome." Vespucci added.

Another maid came in, telling La Donna that it was already ten o'clock. The masseuse was here, as expected. La Donna then excused herself, knowing fully well that it would take at least three hours to get ready. She and Serpina left. Alone at the table, Giachinno felt relieved. Serpina did not suffer at his brother's hands.

Chapter 18

The party-goers began arriving as early as four o'clock, even though the invitation said five. One of the reasons was that carriage lines proceeded slowly. Passengers, dressed in their cumbersome costumes, took forever to disembark from their vehicles. In true 18th century protocol, one did not just jump out of the carriage even if they were just a few feet short of the entrance. For one thing, it was a breach of etiquette. It was also a physical impracticality. The carriages were too high and a footman was needed to either provide a step or pull out the one built in under the carriage.

When the passengers disembarked, they would present their invitation to the guardsman, who would then give it to a footman. The footman would escort the person (or persons,) to the ballroom. The footman presented the invitation to the crier, who in turn announced the arrival of said guest (or guests.) The invitee was able to make a grand entrance, and her attendance would be noted by those already there. The other reason was that the next day, the host's secretary would be handed these invitations, so as to write cards of thanks to those who did attend.

The Marchese di Tursi made a rare appearance. He had abandoned Palazzo di Tursi to take up residence in Fiuggi, as prescribed by his doctor. Fiuggi was and still is, known for its baths. The Marchese had suffered greatly from gout and urinary problems, so he headed south with his wife and a small entourage to find treatment in its therapeutic waters, which were known to be particularly beneficial. He had built a small but elegant house there, so incredibly comfortable that he rarely came to Florence anymore.

He did not favor parties, but given that this was for a good cause, he acquiesced. By his side was his wife La Donna Claudia di Tursi, looking regal in her ball gown of green silk taffeta. The orchestra played as the guests kept coming in. Servants rushed in and out, carrying enough platters of hors d'ouvres and canapés to feed a small battalion.

It wasn't only a ball. It was also an opportunity for mischief among the many young men who attended. This was an opportunity to meet with lovers, perhaps disappear for a while in the Palazzo grounds. No one would be wiser.

Meanwhile, the older women had come for totally different reasons. To be seen, to be talked about, to talk about others. Stuck in boring and in most cases loveless marriages, their neuroses were somewhat assuaged by these celebrations. The older men got to drink themselves silly while the middle aged women, especially the unmarried ones, got to flirt shamelessly with anyone.

Perhaps that's why masked balls were so popular. With a mask on, the person became more of oneself. With a physical mask on, the intangible mask came off, revealing a less inhibited and repressed person.

Serpina stood on the periphery of the dance floor, close to the side of the orchestra. She didn't need someone to ask her to dance. She didn't need to eat or drink. Just to be in a ball gown, standing there, was already magical. When news of her invitation was made known, all the female servants rushed to ask her if it was really true. If it were anyone but Serpina, the servants would have cut her down with malicious remarks. But Serpina was loved by all. In fact, when she had finished attending to her mistress and given leave, a majority of the female staff rushed to her room to help or gaze at her in her attire, offering kind or encouraging words. The first time Serpina was offered a tray, she merely shook her head. She was too excited to eat. A couple of younger gentlemen approached her, asking her to dance, but she merely thank them and said no.

Suddenly, the music stopped. A large group of people, presumably the chorus, assembled behind the musicians, getting ready to perform the oratorio.

An oratorio was a musical presentation of a religious nature. It tells the story of a biblical character with text from scripture. Jacobo L'Abbate had chosen the story of "David". He had written the classical piece with a baroque flair. Despite the popularity of the piano-forte, Jacobo insisted that a harpsichord be included, adding a suggestion of Jacobo's love for Bach.

When the chorus was finally in place, the people began to clap as an elegant and handsome man began to make his way to the orchestra. It was none other than Giaochinno Vespucci, dressed elegantly in a richly embroidered pale blue and gold coat. He acknowledged their applause with a slight bow, which made them clap even louder. After a little while, the crowd began to quiet down. Jacobo looked at Vespucci, who gave a little nod. Jacobo turned to the orchestra and raised his arms, baton in one hand. Suddenly, the orchestra came alive, and the conversation died down. The orchestra played a few more measures when Vespucci opened his mouth, filling the ballroom with the purest, clearest soprano voice ever heard.

Vespucci sang the opening number, a rather complicated piece where David (the shepherd boy) praised God for blessing him abundantly, the text taken from Psalm 19.

"The heavens declare the glory of God;

And the firmament sheweth his handiwork."

This particular song would utilize a soprano, chorus and orchestra. Three of the best pieces, all sung by Vespucci, were selected for the night's preview. The entire oratorio was actually an hour and a half long, too long for such a crowd as this. So the recital was perfect. The whole oratorio was to be performed later in the week at the Cathedral, where many of the night's attendees would surely be absent.

The crowd was awed. For some, this was the first time they heard the castrato, and they were short of amazed. The last piece, which was also the last song in the oratorio, was done in *'presto con brio'* (at a very fast tempo; with liveliness). It was a song of victory and celebration. The shepherd boy had just slain the giant Goliath with his sling. He also had (using one's imagination) just chopped the colossal head off. Vespucci ran through the elaborate and complicated notes as precise as a machine. Finally, the chorus, in canon fashion, sang the theme underneath as Vespucci sang higher and higher, finally hitting the "D" above high "C" and holding it for nearly half a minute. The crowd went wild. They applauded the Castrato, calling out bravo and bravissimo. Many of the women threw flowers at his feet, yelling his name. One woman, a lady of the court, was heard to scream "Vespucci is proof there is a God!" She promptly swooned and had to be carried out for some air.

The mass started to shout for more. "Encore! Encore!" but Vespucci knew that to keep them wanting more, he should give them less. He bowed again, raised Jacobo's hand in triumph. He turned to present the orchestra, the first chair accepting his handshake with humility. The members of the string section tapped their bows noisily against their stands, while the other musicians chose to use their hands in lieu of damaging their instruments. Vespucci took one last bow, made his way through the throng and disappeared. The ball resumed.

"La Donna Abriana must be so proud," Dottore Tebaldi said as he came up to her. She nearly didn't recognize him because of the mask he wore.

"Dottore Tebaldi, how good of you to come."

"I couldn't miss that!" the doctor gesticulated wildly.

"So tell me, Dottore, does hearing an angel sing warrant a good enough pledge from you for our beloved *L'ospedale?*"

"But of course, La Donna."

"Shall we say a thousand lire?" Abriana teased him, hoping that the other gentlemen surrounding her would be goaded into pledging too.

"Please, La Donna, angels do not come cheap. I will pledge five thousand lire."

The gentlemen congratulated him as a few heads turned. In a minute, the news that Tebaldi was pledging *'cinque mille'* had spread all over, prompting the other scions to match or top the offer. The lady who swooned had revived. When she heard the Tebaldi proposal, she went straight to La Donna Abriana and told her to send someone to pick up her pledge of six thousand lire, if

Vespucci would do the honors of lunching with her. Abriana accepted on his behalf, knowing her fiancé's philanthropic nature.

Serpina was mesmerized. She had heard the rumors of 'The Voice'. When she finally heard it, her astonishment was complete. Seeing Vespucci leave, she felt the night to be complete. Nothing else more magnificent would be forthcoming. She did not want the night to end, but at the same time she decided to retire, knowing that the night was now complete. She had her memories, which she would replay a thousand times. She left through one of the side doors, the one that would take her to the back through a side garden, hardly used by anyone.

Chapter 19

La Donna had secured a small salon, prior to the ball, for Giaochinno. She knew that he would need a place of solitude after the performance, as was his usual practice. However, when she made her way to the room, she was shocked to see the door wide opened and a stream of people coming in and out. She stood outside the hall, unsure of what to do about all the admirers. Still standing in the hallway, out of the corner of her eye, she spied the majordomo of the house giving directions to one of the footmen. She made his way to him. The steward of the house smiled when he saw her. She stood close to him, whispered something in his ear, to which he nodded that he understood. Abriana had told him to 'diplomatically' get these people out. With that done, Abriana joined her beloved.

Giaochinno was sitting on a love seat, still wearing his costume, smiling and nodding to the well-wishers, thanking people who descended upon him like ants to a dying insect. Abriana sat next to him.

"Another resounding success, I would say."

"Grazie, Donna Abriana." Gio said, as another well-wisher came up to him to pay his respects.

"You don't seem too thrilled."

"I am. I just don't understand what happened to Vincenzo. He was supposed to be here."

"I'm sure he'll show up when he decides too." An old lady in a blood red ball gown approached the couple. She wore a tiara and practically dripped in jewels. People made way for her. Vespucci tried to remember her name, Contessa something or another, but her name escaped him. 'Contessa Ricci', that was it, he told himself. Vespucci stood up.

"Ah, my dear boy. You brought so much joy with your gift."

"Grazie, my dear Contessa, molto grazie." Abriana was about to stand when the Contessa gestured her to stay seated.

"No, my dear Donna Abriana. You don't need to stand up on my account."

The Contessa began to fan herself. They made small talk as the room began to clear a bit. "So, Signor Vespucci, will you be staying in Florence long? I hear you travel to and fro."

"I may stay awhile, but I have engagements in Paris and London to begin the season."

"A pity. Still, I know how busy your life must be. I just wanted to tell you how much I enjoyed tonight's performance."

"Your ladyship is too kind."

"Well, I must go. I should remember to pay my respects to your father, the Marchese and his wife." Vespucci managed a slight bow.

As the Contessa turned to leave, Giaochinno spotted Vincenzo entering the room.

"As I was saying Gio, you shouldn't be too sad about your brother's absence."

Giaochinno saw Vincenzo approach him.

"Ah, I am sad no longer," Giaochinno smiled widely.

"La Donna Abriana di Tursi, allow me to present to you my most esteemed brother, Signor Vincenzo Vespucci." Gio gestured with his hands.

Abriana looked up.

"But of course!" Abriana stood up. "It is a pleasure to finally meet the elusive Signor Vincenzo Vespucci," she said as she curtsied.

Vincenzo executed a formal bow and said "Your Ladyship."

"So Gio, where *do* you think Vincenzo has been?" Abriana asked. Giaochinno was about to reply when he heard Vincenzo say, "I've been here and there," Vincenzo answered.

"Vincenzo travels a lot," Giaochinno added.

"I see," Abriana said.

"La Donna Abriana is very beautiful. What do you think, Giaochinno?"

"My Abriana is the sweetest, most beautiful woman in Florence."

"Why, thank you, and I thought you haven't noticed," Abriana said.

"Giaochinno notices everything. And everyone." Vincenzo offered.

"I only notice the beautiful." Gio responded.

"That's so sweet of you," Abriana fanned herself.

"So, you're marrying my brother. Have you slept with her yet, Giaochinno?"

"What?" Giaochinno looked at Vincenzo, shocked. His question punctuated by the clatter of a tray carried by a servant.

"Oh, dear, the Contessa! Excuse me, Gio." Abriana stood up quickly and left to see if the old lady was all right.

"Vincenzo, do you have to be vulgar? This is the woman who I am marrying. I would kindly request you to please show her respect."

"Women know only this kind of respect." Vincenzo held his crotch and laughed. "See how she respects me. She didn't even ask if I was enjoying myself," Vincenzo pouted.

"You can be such an ass." Gio accused him.

"She hates me. She thinks I'm a freak, just like you." With that said, Vincenzo turned and left the room, an upset Giachinno following him.

"Where are you going? You just got here." Gio pleaded.

"I need some air. These events make me suffocate."

The pair went through a pair of French doors that led to a side garden. Giaochinno spotted Serpina, sitting on a stone bench.

"Ah, well, well, well. Who do we have here?" Vincenzo asked feigning surprise.

Serpina stood up. "Signor Vespucci!" She said surprised.

"Serpina" Giaochinno noted.

"Our little Serpina!" Vincenzo added. "If I may, Signor. I wanted to say thank you." "Thank you, for what?" Vincenzo asked.

"For giving me the opportunity to hear you perform, Signor Vespucci."

"Mi piacere. My pleasure, Miss Serpina."

"Now I know why people flock to see you. I have listened to some music before, but yours…yours was…" she stopped, trying to find the words. "God, you are so boring." Vincenzo sat on the opposite bench. "I have listened to music before, Signor." Vincenzo mimicked Serpina maliciously.

Serpina put her hand over her chest.

"I must be going, Signor." Serpina pulled up the skirt of her gown and began to walk.

"Serpina!" Giacochinno called after her. The girl stopped and turned.

"Don't leave. I wanted to tell you that, ah, that what you heard was a, ah--a joke. We were just joking."

"Joking, Signor?" Serpina looked bewildered. "Yes. It's just a joke."

"I don't think it was 'just a joke' as you might state it, Signor. I have never heard anything more real in my life." She said. Just as tears began to well in her eyes, she fled.

"Serpina," Vincenzo stood up and called after her, "come back! I forgot tell you how insipid you are!"

When she didn't return, Vincenzo sat down again. He stretched his legs, raised his arms and produced a yawn.

"God, she's such a simpleton."

"I want you to stay away from her." Giaochinno said.

"From the maid?" Vincenzo snorted.

"You heard me."

"I can do what I want, you can't stop me."

"Please Vincenzo, she is innocent."

"Innocent? How can you stand there and claim she is innocent?"

"She didn't know," Giaochinno said, resigned.

"She could have known if she cared enough to ask. Did she ask, Giaochinno?"

"No, but..."

"Basta! Enough," Vincenzo snarled. "I am beginning to question your allegiance, Giaochinno. First you chose music over me. Then you chose the bitch."

"It isn't about choosing sides, Vincenzo!"

"Signor Vespucci." A voice called out. "Signor

Vespucci?"

"Here!" Both of them answered.

A footman appeared. "Scusi, Signor, but there is a man at the servants' entrance demanding to see you."

"Probably some bastard faggot who wants your autograph, Gio." Vincenzo scornfully remarked.

"He said it was of the utmost importance, Signor." The footman announced.

"Everything is so bloody important," Vincenzo said. "Probably another idiot with a passion for freaks."

"Well, who is it?" Giaochinno asked impatiently. The footman looked uncomfortable.

"He says he is Signor Lorenzo Vespucci, your father."

Chapter 20

The years had not been kind to Lorenzo Vespucci. When the boys left, Gabriella was inconsolable, withdrawing more and more each day. Lorenzo tried to cheer her up, buying her that new dress as he had promised. Gabriella wondered where the money came from, so Enzo finally confessed to the meeting he had with Gaspari. She tore the dress, all the while calling him inhumane. She said he was a slave trader, a monster. She called him every name in the book, and fell sobbing. From that day on, she ceased speaking to Enzo. Enzo didn't care. He had money now. He went on a binge, spending his new wealth on games of chance, alcohol and loose women.

Gabriella went back to selling fish, if only to save enough money for train passage to visit her sons. Annunziata had another stroke and finally died exactly one month after the twins' departure. Enzo, feeling some remorse at his debauchery and needing to assuage his guilt, spent the last of the money on her funeral. He bought the most expensive casket and even hired a band to play as they lowered the coffin into the ground. As soon as the crowd dispersed, Enzo headed straight back to the tavern, to be consoled by his friends who knew he would be in a buying mood.

Gabriella, feeling abandoned and utterly hopeless, decided that there was nothing left in San Gimignano for her. She knew her sons were in L'Aquila. Still, she felt uncomfortable of traveling to a place where she knew no one. Her indecision was remarkably changed though one day when she met Signora Conti at the market. Her old neighbor had just returned from her honeymoon from Florence.

Signora Conti had ceased pining for her old lover and accepted a marriage proposal from a wealthy merchant who spoiled her.

She was so happy to see Gabriella. After inquiring about her health, Conti launched into a monologue of everything she did in Florence.

One thing that astounded her was a man who sang like a woman at the opera they had attended. She then began to talk about these men, repeating the gossip about how the 'Castrato' came to be.

Signora Conti stopped when she saw Gabriella turn white. She then silently cursed herself at her stupidity. Gabriella turned and ran all the way home. She packed what she owned in a small suitcase and began walking quickly, almost running. She walked for miles in the muddy road that she believed would lead to L'Aquila and the Palazzo Gaspari. Finally, near the point of exhaustion, a covered wagon stopped. It looked like it was about to rain again.

Lightning flashed as thunder rumbled close by.

"Where are you going?" asked the driver, who scrutinized her from head to foot. Although she felt uncomfortable with his gaze, her panic and weariness from walking made her answer him.

"L'Aquila," she volunteered out of breath.

"Why, that's exactly where we're headed, my friends and I. Why don't you hop in back? There's more than enough room."

"Grazie, Signor," she replied timidly. She had begun to have doubts about the driver. She was a good judge of character, and the man reeked of ill will. Still, she went to the back and took one step up. The first raindrops, huge and pregnant, began to fall. The flap opened as she was about to clamber in. The clouds began to empty themselves.

Before she got in however, she noticed the three men inside. They were unkempt, disheveled with a wild look to them. They stared at Gabriella like hungry wolves studying a poor, lost lamb. She froze in mid-step.

"You know, I forgot something, I have to go back," she cautiously stepped back down. One by one the men came out of the wagon. The raindrops splattered to the ground.

"Leaving so soon?" one said.

"You can't leave yet," the other one snarled.

Gabriella tried valiantly to apologize for inconveniencing them, tried to explain that she forgot something very important and needed to go back. The third man lunged at her. She stepped aside as he tried to grab her. Although he was unsuccessful, he still managed to hang on to her dress, ripping the left sleeve. Two of the men laughed and they began to chase her. Like a cat playing with an insect, the four men (the driver had joined in) drew a circle around her and began to push her to and fro.

"Please! Please. You need to let me go. I have to see my children."

"So you're not a virgin?" laughed one of the men.

"Please, I need to see them. They're in danger. They're all I have." She cried, her tears mingling with the rain that fell on her sad face.

"I have money!" she pulled out a handkerchief from

her pocket and untied it. She produced some bills, clutching them, waving it at them.

"If you let me go, I will give you all I have. Please."

One man, the one with a large scar over his pockmarked cheek seized the money and shoved it into his pocket. Another man grabbed her roughly.

All she could hear was laughter and rain.

She struggled, kicking and pleading. They called her a whore and hit her repeatedly. They threw her on the ground. Hands groped her, groping her breasts, pulling at her underwear. Still she fought back. The driver kicked her full force on her side, breaking a rib. When she was doubled in pain, they straightened her out and ripped her dress apart. She screamed as the first man penetrated her. He grunted with each thrust, as the men holding her down egged him on. When he was done with her, the man with the scar took over, then the other, then the other. When they were finished, the three went through her suitcase while the man with the scar beat her face, kicked her again and again, calling her names. Not content with the pain he was inflicting, he took a rock and smashed the right side of her face in.

They left her naked on the side of the road, her meager belongings scattered in all directions. As the rain subsided, Gabriella peered from her undamaged left eye. She noticed the clouds move apart. She saw the face of Jesus in between the clouds, looking at her with infinite sadness. "Please keep my children safe." She intoned. She felt an incredible peace. She would sleep now, she told herself. She would continue her journey when she got some rest. Then she would see her boys, they would be together. She would never let them leave her side again.

She smiled as her spirit left her. The animals came and claimed her body, tearing her limbs and eating her flesh. No one in San Gimignano ever knew.

Enzo eventually ran out of money and sold the only thing of value that he had; the house. He moved in with Grigio where he lived hand to mouth, miserably, for all those years. What made it worse was the fact that recently, everyone talked about San Gimignano's famous son. Giaochinno Vespucci was famous. His father was infamous. People pointed at him, whispering when he passed them by. He knew what they were saying. If your son is so rich, why are you so poor?

He tired of hearing about Giaochinno's success. He lived in Venice and that was too far for him. He didn't have the money, nor the endurance to travel that far. However, he found out that his son was in Florence. That was close by.

Immediately, he went back to Grigio's place, packed his bag and hitched a ride with some peddlers heading for the city. He also stole whatever might be of value that Grigio owned, which was not much to begin with. He hitched a ride with some peddlers who were headed for the city.

***

Giaochinno stood immobile for what seemed a long while. His thought's invaded by his brother's voice.

"What is that bastard doing here?" Vincenzo spat.

"I don't know. I mean, should we see him?" Giaochinno looked around, as if he would find the answer among the plants.

The footman shifted awkwardly on his feet.

"See him? After what he's done to us, selling us like

pigs?"

"He's our father!" Giaochinno implored.

"Signor?" the footman asked.

"That poor excuse of a man was never our father. I don't want to see him ever." Having said that, Vincenzo stood up. He walked to Giaochinno, his face inches from his.

"Kill him," Vincenzo whispered. Giaochinno's eyes widened.

"Are you out of your mind?"

The footman thought of reminding Vespucci again, but thought otherwise.

"If you don't kill him, I will. Mark my words," murmured Vincenzo.

Giaochinno shook his head ever so slowly. The footman cleared his throat.

"Tell the gentleman that Signor Vespucci is otherwise engaged," Giaochinno said.

"Si, Signor." The footman turned to leave.

"Wait!" Giaochinno called after the manservant. "I'll go with you." Giaochinno heard Vincenzo let out a loud groan.

"Si, Signor Vespucci," the footman replied.

"Giaochinno, I am not going with you! I won't! He doesn't deserve to see us." Vincenzo screamed after his brother, but Gio had already left.

The footman led Gio through a maze of hallways, passageways that were used frequently by the servants but never by the residents of the Palazzo. Eventually, the footman brought him through a very busy kitchen. Cooks, assistants and helpers stopped what they were doing, to stare at the celebrity in their midst. They went through another corridor where the major-domo stood waiting by a large door.

"Il Signor need not have come down," the major-domo said. "I would have been more than glad to escort the, ah, gentleman to one of the lesser used salons."

"It's quite alright." Vespucci answered impatiently. "Let him in."

The major-domo nodded to the footman, who in turn opened the smaller door, which was part of the larger door.

"Mi figlio!" the man cried, taking a step over the threshold and embracing Giaochinno, who stood like a statue. Lorenzo took a step back.

"Look at you! So handsome in that coat." Lorenzo gestured with his hands, palms turned up.

"Would the Signor want to convene in my office? It's just down this hall."

"Yes, please," Giaochinno answered weakly.

"This way please, Signor." The major-domo motioned with his hand the direction they needed to take, with the footman heading the way. The steward then opened the door and ushered them in. It was a mid-sized room, with a plain desk and two chairs. Behind the desk, papers were stuffed in little cubbies. Some crates where on the floor, which doubled as a table. There was also a small cot, neatly made. Obviously aside from being his office, it was also his bedroom.

"I will be outside if you need me, Signor," The major-domo announced, as to warn Lorenzo that he would not tolerate any mischief.

"Thank you. This shouldn't take too long." Giaochinno said as he closed the door behind them.

When the door was shut, Giachinno spun around to face his father.

"What are you doing here?" Giaochinno asked hoarsely.

"What?" Lorenzo shrugged, "A father can't see his son?"

"You know what I mean. All these years, not a letter, not a visit."

"What can I say? I've been busy," Lorenzo explained. "I need to work to survive."

"This is not the right place or time to have a discussion. Where are you staying?"

"I was hoping that— " Lorenzo was hoping to be invited to stay at the Palazzo, but Giaochinno knew what he was going to say next.

"Where are you staying?" Giaochinno cut him off.

"There are rooms to let the night, above the Taverna di Osso Negro."

"Taverna di Osso Negro," Giaochinno repeated, to make sure he remembered.

"Si. It's right by the river, on Via Ghirlandaio."
"Alright. There are things I need to attend to. Tomorrow is Saturday. Sunday won't be a good day either.

"Monday, then?" Enzo asked.

"That will be fine. Monday, dinner, say at sundown? I will have my carriage pick you up."

"A carriage? Fine." Enzo was pleased. "Ah, Giaochinno? I was wondering, you know I'm really broke. I only have enough money to--" as he was speaking, Giaochinno pulled out some bills from his inside coat pocket. He took out some notes and placed it on the table.

"That should be enough." Lorenzo stared at the large

bills.

"Oh, yes, Giaochinno, more than enough," he said as he scooped up the bills and put them in his pocket.

Giaochinno stood up and opened the door. He thanked the major-domo for use of his room. Lorenzo exited through the same door, not bothering to say goodbye.

Giaochinno shook his head. His father did not ask about Vincenzo. Not once. It made him sad. When the door shut, he told the major-domo that if he needed anything from the Signor all he had to do was ask. He also said that their business was over. This man was never to be allowed to set foot on Palazzo di Tursi again.

Chapter 21

The foundation of Florence dates back to Roman times. When the oldest part of the city was originated as one of the Caesar's colonies, the city was set between the convergence of its two rivers; the Mugnone and the Arno.

The Arno river flowed west through Florence, finding its way southeast into the Ligurian sea right below the famous city of Pisa, where the leaning tower was located. The Arno river was perhaps one of the reasons that Florence flourished in the earlier days. Trade and the pursuit of commerce thrived on the basis of important routes: land and water. The river brought merchants from the orient; tradesmen, craftsmen and visionaries. The river was life.

Roads were built flanking the Arno as shops, houses and factories sprang up. If one followed the river south by south-west, it would eventually lead to a road called Lungarno del Tiempo, where the Via Ghirlandaio ran perpendicular from it. There, another kind of enterprise grew. The kind of enterprise that was as old as mankind.

The Via Ghirlandaio was named after a lesser known medieval painter. In the daytime, it was a rather ordinary street, with barely a shop or two open. But when darkness fell, the streets began to populate themselves with a more sinister crowd. Prostitutes, both male and female, stood here and there, waiting for a prospect. The bars opened and began to fill with patrons. Con-men eagerly awaited the more gullible visitors. Although many of Florence's gentlemen went there to find a friend, it was not a very friendly place. The more affluent and better dressed tourist would certainly be noticed by its populace, but the young man who was dressed in peasant clothes was not. He wore a cap, low on his head. He had on a jacket, threadbare and worn. He walked within the shadows, quietly but confidently. He glanced up at the rough wooden sign with a black bear crudely painted on it. Underneath, it read "Osso Negro". From inside came laughter and conversation. He waited.

Eventually, a group of three young men approached, not paying him any mind. They opened the door and as they entered, he followed behind them. As he stepped in, the din grew louder. There were a lot of people. He scanned the somewhat busy tavern and found who he was looking for. Now all he had to do was wait. He took a table closest to the door. An obese woman came up to him.

"Well, what do you want?" she asked him in a most vulgar manner.

The clothes had obviously led her to believe that he was a vagrant. She didn't give a second look at his young face, which was grimy and sooty.

Probably some laborer, she thought.

The man asked for a drink. He produced a bill and asked the Signora if this would also be enough to pay for dinner. The woman stuffed the bill down the front of her dress and told him she'd be right out. She came out immediately with a bottle stuck in her armpit, a bowl in one hand and a mug on the other. She placed all of these on the table and left without a word. It was a very busy night for her, and she didn't have time for small talk. The man stared at the wooden bowl. It was filled with what looked like mud. He took the wooden spoon and began to eat ever so slowly.

***

Lorenzo was drunk by now, not noticing the man who watched him intently from behind his low slung cap. In a rare case of foresight, he went ahead and used the money his son gave him to secure three more days (with meals) at the tavern. Then, he used the rest to get sloshed. He was very gallant, buying drinks for the two old men he had befriended. They seemed genuinely interested in his tales, and in the free liquor. The young man tried to hear what they were talking about, but the general noise stifled it. Finally, at about quarter to two, Lorenzo said goodnight to the two old men and went out. The man waited a few seconds, then went out also.

Lorenzo's tiny room was on the second floor. To get there, one had to go out of the tavern and walk behind the building where there was a case of makeshift stairs. He grumbled as he climbed, cursing the stairs for being so steep.

The man waited till he saw Lorenzo enter his room and turn a lamp on. He then went up the stairs himself and knocked softly on the door.

"Who's that?" Lorenzo called from inside.

"Su figlio, Papa."

The door opened a crack and Lorenzo peered out. When he saw who it was, he smiled idiotically.

"Ah! *Mi figlio, mi figlio.*" Lorenzo said as he opened the door. "Come in."

The man took off his cap.

"I didn't want to see you, ever again. But I thought that if I didn't, I would lose this wonderful opportunity to get some satisfaction."

"My son, what are you talking about?" Enzo's smiled disappeared.

"I want you to ask for forgiveness."

"Forgiveness for what?" Lorenzo sneered.

"Forgiveness so that you could live in a palace, so you could eat fine food. Forgiveness for having a servant at your beck and call? Bah! I should be so lucky to ask for such forgiveness."

"I came here hoping that I would find you repentant. I honestly came here thinking that maybe you've changed." The young man shook his head.

"You want me to say I'm sorry? Fine. I'm sorry. I'm very, very…" Enzo was not able to finish his sentence. A hard slap had crossed his face. Then another one. Then a fist. He fell. He felt a kick to his stomach, which made him double over.

"Ah…Papa," the young man said. "Do you know the pain that my brother and I went through? Do you know what it feels like to be stripped and mutilated?"

Lorenzo felt his hands being tied behind him. Then his legs. He was then turned roughly over. A dirty rag was stuffed in his mouth.

"Do you know how it feels to be only half a man?"

He felt the heavy weight of his son's body over him. Face leaning close to his, he whispered "Now you will know."

Lorenzo realized what was about to happen. He tried to scream but only a muffled sound came out. His shirt was torn open. Enzo pissed in his pants. Hands went round his neck, starting to strangle him, but he bucked, hoping to get his assailant off him. Enzo managed only to find the younger man kneeling behind him, lifting his head, pressing a blade to his neck.

"Do you know this knife? You should. It is yours. If

you move, I might just slice you right now and get it over with."

Enzo felt his head lowered to the floor, the drawstring to his pants severed. Then, he was naked, his pants bunched around his ankles. He was looking at the ceiling, praying for mercy, praying for salvation, when his son's face came into view. His son looked deeply into his eyes and said "Like father, like son…."

They found Lorenzo's body the next day. His blood had begun to seep into the floorboards and dripped down into the kitchen below, where the fat cook was sitting, chopping vegetables for the day's entrée. At first she thought a fly had landed on her head. However, the next time she felt it, she brought her hand to her hair and found it wet. She looked up and decided to scream. The neighbors were assembled before the authorities got there. The man was beaten to a pulp, his eyes gouged out, his nipples and genitals sliced off. The news of the grisly murder traveled fast.

Chapter 22

In the year 1814, the corps of *"Carabinieri Reali"* was instituted by royal law. It was both a military and police corps, fighting in every conflict in which Italy was involved, amassing the largest collection of medals in the world for their acts of heroism. In fact, the nickname given to the corps was *'La Benemerita'* or the "well deserving." The first time they appeared in a work of fiction was in Carlo Collodi's "Pinocchio", which created quite a scandal at the time. The fact is that the Carabinieri were much respected and models of serious behavior. One such model was Franco Faldo, a constable of many years.

When he was first summoned to the crime scene, he was expecting a simple case. The residents of this certain district were known to be a reactive bunch. He was certain he would find either a prostitute dead from the hands of a lover, or a lover dead by the hands of a prostitute. Stabbing was the common manner of fatality. However, as he entered the room, his face registered a mixture of shock and disbelief. In all his years as an investigator, Faldo had never witnessed a body so badly mangled.

Asking around, he recorded that the man was one Lorenzo Vespucci, supposed father of the great performer. Faldo put down 'supposedly.' The man was obviously deranged. What would the father of the most famous singer in all of Tuscany and Rome be doing in a place like the Osso Negro?

He interviewed the fat woman who owned the tavern, but all she could add was that the deceased had paid in cash, drank too much and was full of himself. No, he didn't have any visitors. Faldo also questioned those who had a room next door. It was a young girl who claimed to be out all night the previous night. Doing what? She said she worked in a bakery. Faldo knew that she was a prostitute, but did not press her. She would have no information.

Still, Faldo and his assistant left for the Palazzo di Tursi to speak with Il Signor Vespucci. They were escorted to an opulent salon, whose furnishings alone were ten times their salaries combined. They sat and waited, intimidated by the surroundings. Finally, they were escorted to another grander room, where Vespucci sat waiting.

Vespucci was curious as to why they were there but at the same time voiced his opinion that the *Carabinieri* were so vital to the city. This he just mentioned last week to the Director of Justice who was here. Did they know him? The deputy and his assistant shook their heads. Their ranks were so that the highest official they knew was their supervisor's chief. And they had never even met him.

The question demoralized them immediately.

"I'm sorry, gentlemen. I am rambling. Of what service may I be to you?"

"Signor," the assistant began, but was interrupted with a clearing of the throat by the deputy who thought it best that he should be the one to deliver the news. The assistant stopped and did a double take.

"Signor Vespucci. Your father was found dead Sunday morning."

"My father?" Giachinno said, shocked. "That can't be! He was here, the night of the ball. I'm supposed to meet him today!" He sat down, and looked confused.

"He can't be dead! I just talked to him. I mean…" He began to compose himself. "I have not seen my father in nearly fifteen years. I saw him for the first time, Friday night. We met briefly. It was an awkward moment."

"May I ask why, Signor?" Faldo asked.

"I didn't know what to say to him. You can imagine my surprise when he came."

"What did you talk about, Signor?" Faldo inquired.

"Nothing at all, I had a house full of people I was attending to, I was exhausted at having had just performed. So we decided to meet today instead. I was about to have a carriage pick him up." Giaochinno explained.

"You knew where he was staying." Faldo posed it more as a statement than a question.

"But of course. The Taverna di Osso Negro on Via Ghirlandaio. The carriage driver would need an address."

"Of course." The constable nodded.

At that point, La Donna Abriana entered, prompting the officials to stand up. "Gio, caro mio, I just heard."

"Bad news does travel fast," Vespucci shrugged. "La Donna Abriana di Tursi, allow me to present to you…ah, I'm sorry, what were your names?"

The men gave their names, formally bowing to the daughter of the Marchese.

"Signor, one more question," the deputy asked.

"Did your father have any enemies?"

"I wish I knew. Like I said, we barely knew each other."

"I see. We are sorry for your loss," Faldo concluded.

"Thank you," Giaochinno replied without feeling. "You will tell me if this murderer is apprehended?"

"But of course, Signor Vespucci." Both officials nodded.

"Thank you, gentlemen. Thank you very much.

"Someone will see you out." Abriana added.

"Thank you for seeing us." Faldo conceded. With that, they left the room.

"Oh, Gio. Why didn't you tell me your father was here, too? I would have wanted to meet him and pay my respects."

"It was inappropriate. Here comes a man who I haven't seen since God knows when, reeking of alcohol, demanding money. I turned him away."

"Oh my!" Abriana remembered. "We have to tell your brother."

"I am sure that he already knows", he said wearily. He embraced Abriana tightly, and wept quietly.

Outside, Faldo and his assistant spoke briefly about how strange the whole case was. Still, Signor Vespucci was above suspicion. First, he had no motive. Secondly, a man of his distinction would be spotted immediately if he set foot in that street. Thirdly, to even hint that he may be involved would open up a can of worms. Vespucci was rich and powerful. Faldo's career could be squashed by this man with just a few words to the Director. No that wouldn't do. Lorenzo Vespucci's case would never be solved.

Giaochinno did pay for his father's funeral. In true gallant fashion, he also gave the owner of the tavern some money, to cover any other expenses. All this he did through Abriana's secretary, who carried out his instructions explicitly. He did not attend the funeral service. In fact, only the priest, an altar boy and two gravediggers were in attendance on that rainy afternoon. Faldo also went, to check for anything out of the ordinary. By the middle of the service, he realized that this case was over. Without any leads, the file would be delegated to the bottom of a pile that was already too large to begin with. He felt sad, but realized that Lorenzo Vespucci was actually just another drunk who pissed somebody off. Faldo had had seen his share of that.

Chapter 23

Abriana was at a loss. She had tried everything to raise her fiancé's spirits but he remained sullen, uncommunicative and irritable at times. He left for a week, to attend some rehearsal, then came back. It had been two weeks since his father's funeral. When she told him that she would like to accompany him to the funeral, he said that he himself wouldn't go. He hardly knew the man, he replied. Whatever memories he had of him were painful. He had begun to lock himself upstairs, in his bedroom, only to come out for the evening meal the past few days.

Like any other lady of leisure, she had many resources available to her. It was just a question of tapping the right one. She finally had an idea and told her secretary to plan a dinner party for three people. Gio, her and Dottore Tebaldi. She thought herself smart. Her reasoning elegant. The Dottore was highly esteemed in Gio's eyes. The Dottore could possibly prescribe something to aid his depression. The Dottore was always a lot of fun at any social function.

Still, she needed to add one more female. Mrs. Tebaldi could not come. She had left for Milan to visit relatives. Abriana decided to invite her best friend Martina Colon, the same Martina who accompanied her the first time she saw Giaochinno perform. Martina's dizzy nature would provide the necessary comic relief.

She spoke to Serpina about it, needing some validation about her newest enterprise. Serpina assured her that it was a marvelous idea. They spent the next hour discussing (Abriana talking and Serpina nodding and saying 'yes, m'lady' once in while) what was necessary to ensure that her project would be a success.

Abriana thought that three days would be sufficient to create this occasion. She needed a theme. A theme is what would bring everything together. Abriana thought a while and decided that she needed something exotic, mystical and novel. She came up with one; it would be Oriental. She asked Serpina to hand her some stationary and proceeded to make a detailed list of things that had to be obtained, manufactured, bought or done. Before she set anything to paper though, she thought it best to give the guest of honor prior warning. She took a heavier stock of paper and in her fine hand completed an invitation. She requested Serpina to deliver it to Signor. Normally, La Donna would have a male footman take away the invitation, but decided that the maid would be a better envoy. It seemed that her fiancée found the little maid amusing.

In his room, Giaochinno studied his brother.

Vincenzo had his eyebrow raised, as if to ask "what?" He had been quietly civil the last hour, something that was not Vincenzo's usual disposition.

"You killed him."

"No, I did not."

"You killed him, just like you said you would. Now the *Caribinieri* is involved."

"Will you just calm down. God! You are such a little faggot." Vincenzo proceeded to chew the fingernail on his index finger. "What if I did kill him? Don't you think he deserved to die?" Vincenzo smiled.

Just then, a light knock was heard.

"Enter!" Both men said at once. Vincenzo took a seat,

leaving Giachinno standing. The door opened and Serpina came in.

"Aha! Little Serpina, once again." Vincenzo greeted her maliciously.

"*Scusi*, Signor Vespucci."

"Yes, Miss Serpina. We are honored to have you visit." Gio smiled at her.

"Yes, such an honor." Vincenzo mimicked his brother.

"Her ladyship wanted me to give you this." She presented him with a card made of heavy stock.

"Thank you, Serpina."

"*Prego*, Signor." Serpina did a small curtsy.

"Maybe Serpina would like to stay awhile?" Vincenzo suggested.

"Would you like to?" Giaochinno motioned to the chair beside him.

"Oh, no, I couldn't," Serpina answered.

"You just don't want to," Vincenzo accused her. "I don't blame you."

"Thank you for offering, Signor." she said.

"Oh, come on, Serpina. Stay. It'll be like old times," Vincenzo said as he squeezed his breasts in mock fashion.

"I must go now, Signor," Serpina said as she walked toward the door.

"You are such a tease!" yelled Vincenzo.

Just as Serpina was about to turn the doorknob, she stopped. With her hand still at the knob, she turned her head slowly and looked at Giaochinno. "Signor, if I may be so bold," she peered into Gio's eyes, "it would do you well if you got rid of this thing that distresses you so much." Having said her mind, she turned the handle and exited.

"Whore! God damn you!" Vincenzo yelled at the

door.

Giachinno looked at the card. It was an invitation that read like a letter.

"This is to invite Signor…dinner in my honor…Dottore Tebaldi…Martina," Gio read the card.

"I take it I wasn't invited?" Vincenzo asked in mock disappointment.

"I could ask Abriana. She knows you are in and out. That's why she probably--"

"I wouldn't ask that slut for anything if my life depended on it," Vincenzo snarled.

"Vincenzo! I told you not to do that!"

"Go to your party," Vincenzo said angrily. "I won't be there! In fact, I'm leaving you. Maybe for good. Maybe I'll never come back. Then you'll be all alone. All alone Gio. Think about that."

Chapter 24

When La Palazzo di Tursi was built, the architect made sure there were enough rooms for dining and entertaining. There was the great hall, which could easily fit two to three hundred people. Then there was the lesser hall, which had a capacity half of its larger sibling. In addition, there was the formal dining room, which could only sit a pitiful thirty or forty guests. Finally, there was the family dining room that held about 12 to 15 people. None of these rooms were to be used for this exceptional affair. Instead, La Donna had a structure built specially for it. It was a miniature, three story pagoda, painted red and green and gilded in gold. It was created from a lithograph that Abriana found in a book on the Far East. Lacking color though, she told the master carpenter to use his imagination, which he did. Hundreds of little paper lanterns hung from its eaves, while silk flags of matching red and gold waved from spindly poles that surrounded it. The interior was an octagonal space, not very large, perhaps about twenty feet in diameter. But what it lacked in size it made up in sumptuousness. A low lacquered table sat in the center, surrounded by large, overstuffed pillows in dark red damask with gold trim. From the ceiling down to the floor hung yards and yards of alternating pale green silk and dark green velvet. Eight huge celadon vases stood in attention in each corner of the room, with palm trees as its background. The floor was covered in plain, woven mats. There was not enough time to tile it.

Serpina found herself and four other maids sewing robes of green and gold velvet for the servers who would be attending the small group. The first designs that were given to her were of Persian origin, with Abriana explaining that the Chinese costume she found in a publication too plain. Serpina suggested the merging of the styles of the two dynasties, to which La Donna thought was brilliant.

Finally the day of the dinner arrived. Two footmen, wearing Serpina's creation, escorted the somewhat cheerless Signor Vespucci to the pagoda. Abriana, Dottore Tebaldi and Martina were waiting for him already. Despite his gloom, Giaochinno managed to smile and act jovial, if only for the sake of his guests and all the hard work they put into this event.

He sat on a cushion, there were no chairs, and found it comfortable even though strange. He praised Abriana for her graciousness. Martina complained that she and Dottore Tebaldi contributed too, in one way or another, their efforts to the project. He commended them too. A diminutive, oriental woman sat a little ways from them and proceed to play a string instrument that sang a relaxing, haunting melody. It reminded Vespucci of a muted harpsichord.

When they were all seated, the servants began their parade. A procession of culinary delights were set on the table before them. Tiny morsels of steamed, seasoned pork, savory ground beef and shrimp, all wrapped in a shimmering wrapper of rice. Other delectable bits and bite size pieces came at them. Then, the sorbet. A small amount of shaved ice with a hint of lemon and sweetness. The amazing thing about the sorbet was how it was served. Each serving of sorbet was placed in the hollowed back of a large swan, sculpted in ice.

When the sorbet was cleared, platters of seafood arrived next. Shiny black mussels in garlic, oysters, squid and scallops. A large grouper, the size of a small child, was brought in on a large platter, steaming of lemon grass and sesame oil. This time around, the sorbet was served inside a miniature pagoda about a foot tall, also carved in ice. To get to the sorbet, the roof had to be detached. The dinner was a dazzling array of variety. One didn't feed. One took a small bite of what was offered and savored its complex taste. Then one moved on to the next item. They chatted about this and that, Dottore Tebaldi being a wonderful conversationalist. Martina did prove to be her impractical self, lending hilarious insight in an adorable way. They talked about the arts and the fulfillment it brought not only to the audience but to the players themselves.

Dottore Tebaldi, an amateur actor in his younger years said that acting was an act of giving one's self. Abriana was struck with an idea. Her mother, an avid of the arts and stage, would be celebrating her birthday in a few weeks. Abriana had fretted on what gift would be appropriate. She had already commissioned a jeweler to create a marvelous pair of earrings. However, she felt that this was not good enough. She thought frankly that the wife of the Marchese could buy any jewelry she'd want. She was intrigued at the premise of what Dottore Tebaldi said and asked for clarification.

"Well, to perform on stage, one needs to act well. To act well, one must take a part of himself and transmit that to the audience."

"What part?" Martina asked.

"The part that remains hidden but each possesses. One's soul." The good dottore punctuated the end of his statement with a flourish of his fork, which still had a shrimp stuck to it.

"But how do you give your soul away?" Martina asked again, sincerely believing the question to be valid. "I mean, if that's the case then I shall be exempt. I sold my soul years ago." They all laughed at her joke.

"My dear Martina, you have a beautiful soul." Gio said.

"So do you, Signor Vespucci," Martina countered.

"Acting brings out not only the beauty of each soul," continued Tebaldi, "but all the wounds and pain. It brings out all the fears and joys. The actor takes all this and offers it, he becomes connected to the audience in a way that transcends all logic and reason. Although many actors I have spoken to will swear there was that connection."

"This fascinates you, Donna mia?" Vespucci noticed Abriana listening attentively, face enraptured.

"Well, yes," she replied. "My mother is having a birthday. What better gift than to put on a play for her!"

"My dear, I am a singer," Gio explained. "Not an actor."

"Bah!" Tebaldi dismissed him. "Opera is singing while acting, although I've seen some operas where the performers where more actors than singers." They all laughed again.

Martina thought it would be a good idea. "I've always wanted to be an actress." She added, "I think I would be pretty good."

"Really, Miss Martina?" Tebaldi asked.

"When I was married to my last husband, (God rest his soul), I used to act every night." She howled, laughing at her own joke. Seeing Martina express amusement with such abandon made them laugh with her.

"It would be a fine present," Tebaldi announced.

"I was thinking of asking you to write it for us Dottore Tebaldi," Abriana asked.

"Hmm, I think that I could come up with something. I wrote many plays when I was a student. I managed to keep most of them."

"Wait…"Martina said, remembering something. "It has to be about the Greeks, your mother loves the Greeks."

"Ah, yes." Abriana remembered how engrossed her mother was with tales of gods and goddesses, myths and legends. She had traveled to Greece on more than one occasion.

"Perhaps a comedy?" Martina recommended.

"A tragedy," Vespucci said darkly.

"Yes! Lovers, doomed," Tebaldi contributed gaily.

"Romance," Abriana sighed.

"And betrayal," Giaochinno added.

"Bravo!" Tebaldi said. "I have just the play! It was one of the last ones that I wrote. Let me bring it tomorrow and you can see if it will do."

They all agreed to meet for tea at Martina's, since she needed the opportunity to show off the beautiful garden she had just put in.

They went on to discuss other things for 'their' play as they began dessert. Giaochinno's mood improved. For a little while, he was his old self again, scarcely giving a thought to his brother.

Chapter 25

The next day, Abriana and Giaochinno took a carriage across the bridge, to visit Martina. Martina Colon lived in a spacious town house on Via del'Nelli, which was just a few steps from the Duomo square and the Cappelle Medici. It was an expensive piece of real estate, but Martina was well off. She had married young to a wealthy man who died in an equestrian accident. He had the foresight to write a will and leave her everything. She remarried another gentleman of equal prosperity. He died too, this time from a stroke. Martina thought herself to be unlucky with husbands and swore she would never marry again.

She met another young gentleman who was healthy, not very rich but comfortable. He lasted barely a year when he joined the army to fight and died in battle. From then on, Martina took on lovers at night and filled her days with whatever distractions she might find. She once complained that she was lucky in cards and unlucky in love, a detail she proved true many times over in any of the gambling houses she'd visited.

Her current diversion was her garden. The town house didn't have one. What it did have was a small, enclosed space behind the house. It was bare, except for an old well that stood forlorn in the south corner. Martina consulted with a few friends who referred her to a man who did landscaping. In a few weeks, the boring space became a showcase of foliage and vegetation. Martina herself did not have a green thumb, but she had the money to pay a gardener to tend to it daily, so the shrubbery always looked there best. It was in this very garden that the foursome met. A small table was set up, and high tea was served. Serpina, ever faithful, was on hand and helped in the service.

Tebaldi proudly produced a thin manuscript and proceeded to tell them the story.

"I wrote this play when I was in Greece, when I was a young man of twenty. It happens to be, among other things, a tragedy."

"A tragedy?" Martina whined. "That means someone dies. I don't like it."

Tebaldi looked at Martina, undecided as to whether she was finding humor or was serious. "Excuse me, Dottore, but I concur with Martina. Why a tragedy? Why does someone have to die?" Abriana wished she had paid more attention to her tutors.

"You see a tragedy brings the hero or heroine through suffering, often to the moment of their death so they might achieve insight into a higher law, beyond human understanding."

"I see…" Abriana said as she took a sip of her tea.

"I don't," Martina pouted.

"I think, Martina dearest, what Doctor Tebaldi means to say is that our awareness of death is finite and restricted," Giaochinno added.

"Exactly," Tebaldi remarked excitedly.

"So someone has to die?" Martina made a face.

"Not exactly. Death can take many forms. Not merely a physical death, although that is the most visual." Tebaldi stood up. "Death can also be the separation of a soul from God, or that soul losing its humanity or identity."

"That seems rather profound," Abriana commented, fanning herself.

"All tragedy is profound," Giachinno said, patting his lips with a linen napkin.

"But why?" Martina whined. "I mean why would people want to watch tragedies? I mean, so much sadness."

"Well, Miss Martina, I will answer you that by telling you what tenets makes up a tragedy."

"Tenets?"

"Like a set of guidelines, Martina dearest." Abriana explained, patting her best friend's hand.

"Oh. All right," Martina was resigned that they were not going to do a comedy.

"There are four," Tebaldi started. "The first one being that a true tragedy must have a hero who is good and revered. Someone admirable."

"I think he should be bad. So when he dies, the people will applaud at the end." Martina clapped her hands.

"That's precisely why the hero must be good. A bad man's downfall results in the audience cheering. As Aristotle says, the fall of an essentially good person disturbs us. It stirs within us pity and compassion. In fact, the nobler the hero is, the greater our grief or anxiety when he loses his soul."

"I see." Martina nodded slowly. "Yes, that does make sense."

"Which brings us to the second tenet," Tebaldi continued. "A true tragedy must evoke in the audience fear and disappointment. They must pity the hero. As Aristotle points out, fear and pity becomes a catharsis, a cleansing of our emotions."

"Oh, like how I felt when I saw Aida get buried with what-his-name," Martina exclaimed.

"Radames," Vespucci came to the rescue.

"That's the man," Martina agreed.

"What about Aida?" Abriana asked.

"Well," Martina began, "when I knew they were both going to die, I felt really disappointed. I was hoping for a happy ending. Then, when we left the opera house, I felt…I don't know, like I was relieved."

"Precisely. That was the catharsis that Aristotle was speaking of," Tebaldi smiled.

"Oh…" Martina was awed with her new found enlightenment.

"I'm sorry Dottore, please continue." Martina realized that she was holding up the conversation.

"Which brings us to the third tenet. The hero's demise must come about because of some error in decision, a product of a fatal choice."

"Which makes the hero not an innocent victim, but someone responsible for his own doom," Vespucci added.

"So genuine tragedy," Abriana ventured, "doesn't occur because of bad luck or blind accident. Would that be a correct assumption?"

"Yes, La Donna Abriana. I see that the ladies are not only beautiful, but highly intelligent as well," Tebaldi smirked.

Vespucci said 'hear, hear' as Abriana blushed and Martina guffawed most unlady like.

"Wait a minute, you said there were four?" Martina stopped in mid laugh.

"That was very observant of you Miss Martina. The fourth one is the simplest. A true tragedy must have a dynamic contest between two opposing forces."

"Good versus the bad?" Abriana questioned.

"Not necessarily. It could be good versus good," Tebaldi said.

"How can good battle itself?" Martina pondered the last statement.

"Strictly speaking, the most tragic of all confrontation is when good is up against good and the contest is to the death."

A collision of two values," Giaochinno added.

"I still can't see how good can fight good," said Martina.

"Let's see." Tebaldi put his hand on his chin.

"Maybe I can give you a good example." Abriana and Martina remained respectively silent as Tebaldi contemplated. "Ah. Let us suppose you are a magistrate. Your daughter is brutally raped which led her to suicide. But because of legalities, the man is set free. What do you do? Abriana?" Abriana pursed her lips.

"I wouldn't be able to do anything. I would bear the sadness, most definitely," she concluded.

"And how about you, Miss Martina?"

"I would take justice into my own hands. I would hunt that man down and kill him." Martina grasped a butter knife and plunged it into a container of butter.

"Martina!" Abriana scolded her lightly.

"Aha! That is exactly good versus good. To do nothing is good in the eyes of some. To have revenge is good in the eyes of others." Tebaldi concluded.

"As usual, Dottore, you have brought us illumination," Giaochinno was apparently impressed.

"So, a tragedy it will be then." Martina finally assented.

"I will have copies of the play made and I will send it

to you. Meanwhile, we may go over the points of this drama."

"Who do I play?" Martina asked excitedly.

"Ah, Martina, you will be a goddess. Abriana will be the woman who is madly in love with our Greek youth." Tebaldi looked at Vespucci pitifully. "Giaochinno will be our tragic hero."

Chapter 26

Because of their schedules, Tebaldi urged the players to memorize their lines by themselves. They would only have a few rehearsals where all of them could be assembled. Martina and Abriana had more of an occasion to get together, with Serpina reading the lines of the men. Thankfully, Serpina's father was a scholar who taught her how to read at a very young age.

Giacchinno, on the other hand, had to leave for Rome. A new pope, Pius VIII, had just been elected and the Prefect of the Apostolic office had written him, inviting him to the new pope's coronation. He wrote back, accepting the honor and directly packed his bags.

Giaochinno felt very much alone in Rome, missing Abriana. He also missed Vincenzo terribly, but was hopeful that his brother would feel the same way and return. So he busied himself with rehearsals and various functions. The coronation came and went. The Prefect was more than grateful and hinted that Vespucci's notable fealty to the church was not unnoticed. On his second last night in Rome, he visited an old friend who persuaded him to stay in his villa. Vespucci agreed, desperate for some form of companionship.

He traveled back to Florence, but soon found himself alone in Palazzo di Tursi. He was informed that La Donna Abriana had gone to Venice, to attend a funeral of one Contessa Ursula Ricci. Giaochinno suddenly realized it was the lady in the red gown whom he had met at the ball. How fragile life was, he thought. Giaochinno then thought of following Abriana to Venice, but weary of travel, decided against it. Instead, he spent the day memorizing his lines for the play. She should be back tomorrow or the day after, he was assured, so it didn't make sense for him to leave.

That very evening, Giaochinno couldn't sleep. He tossed and turned in his bed, not able to place the source of his anxiety. The night was so cool that he left the shuttered doors that led to the balcony wide open. He heard the wind rustle the leaves of the large olive tree beside the balcony. The continuous whisper finally affected him and he found himself drowsy. His body jerked as Vincenzo's voice came to him from the balcony.

"Wake up, brother. I need you." He heard Vincenzo say.

Giaochinno sat up, startled.

"You came back!" Gio whispered, elated.

"Your love brought me back," sobbed Vincenzo.

Was his brother crying? "I didn't want to come back. I didn't want to." Giaochinno saw his brother's outline against the moonlight.

"But you did because you know that I need you." Gio cried too. He stood up and approached his brother.

"Gio." He embraced his brother and kissed him full in the mouth, without malice. Giaochinno took both hands and held his brother's face.

"Vincenzo, don't ever leave me," Gio said as he began to kiss his brother's eyes, cheeks and forehead. "I am not complete without you."

"Yet time and again you choose them over me," Vincenzo said as he wiped Giaochinno's eyes with his sleeve.

"Because you have so much poison in you," Giaochinno said tenderly, then added, "You must learn to forgive."

That one word changed Vincenzo's whole demeanor instantaneously.

"Forgive?" Vincenzo said angrily. "There is no forgiveness in my heart. They took what was most important to me, Gio. You of all people must realize this."

"But there is nothing else we can do," Gio explained.

"There is much I can do. Revenge, for one thing. Revenge to the people who did this to me."

"Vincenzo, they didn't know any better."

"There you go again. Choosing them over me."

"What would you want me do? Go on a killing spree?"

"Yes!" Vincenzo roared. "Kill them, each and every one of them. Gaspari, Bragantti, Titino…" he paused and looked at Giachinno.

"Gabriella Vespucci," he whispered, his voice taking on a most unnatural growl.

"No…" Giachinno took a step back, as if pushed.

"You know where they all are. Hunt them down like the dogs they are. Then kill them."

"No, Vincenzo. Forgive. Forgive...forgive" he fell on his knees and hugged his brother's knees.

"You are a weak fool. Weak and spineless."

"And what about my soul?" Giachinno cried out loud. Vincenzo pulled him up and grasped his arms.

"Your soul would be lost. Like mine already is."

"No…please Vincenzo. Don't ask me to do this." He embraced his brother again, much like a drowning man would embrace a life vest.

"If you love me like you say you do, then I need not even ask you," Vincenzo said.

"Then why do you, Vincenzo? Why do you ask this of me?"

"Because it is proof of our oneness. If you do not, then you are against me. If you are against me, then I want no part of you."

"Vincenzo, I cannot."

"Then you are my enemy. I will treat you as such."

Gio finally released his hold on his brother and stood, undecided. Finally, he looked at his brother and said in a small voice, "I will do it."

"Good," Vincenzo pronounced it slowly. "What will you do?"

"I will kill them."

"Kill who?"

"Gaspari, Bruno, Titino…" he repeated in a daze.

"And?"

"No…" he began to whimper softly.

"And?"

"That I cannot do!" he fell on his knees again. Vincenzo kneeled also, each man face to face. "She should be the very first one."

"She didn't know, Vincenzo."

"A mother would know."

"But she didn't. She didn't do anything…"

"By doing nothing she allowed this to happen!"

"She is blameless!"

"Is she?"

***

The footman entered Vespucci's room early the next morning to draw the bath and to wake the Signor for his morning tea. He found the famous singer on the floor, bedclothes in a tangle. He gently tapped the man.

"Signor Vespucci? Signor, are you alright?" he asked with great concern. Giaochinno woke up and placed his hands on his face.

"Signor, would you like me to call for the physician?"

Giaochinno shook his head.

"No," he mumbled. "No. I'm fine." He stood up shakily, with the footman's help. He sat on the chair.

"Signor, if I may, I think that I should call the physician. You do not look well."

Vespucci shook his head and raised his hand.

"I was probably sleep walking. Don't worry yourself. I will be fine."

"As you wish, Signor."

"Thank you for your concern, really. I would appreciate it if you do not mention this ah, episode to anyone."

"But of course, Signor."

The footman finished his chores. He asked Vespucci if there was anything else and then was dismissed. The footman exited, closing the door softly behind him. The footman had noticed the knife on the floor, beside Vespucci when he first came in. It had a dark wooden handle that had some kind of carving. Despite his promise, he would tell Serpina about it. Serpina would tell him what to do. He shook his head, not knowing what to think.

Chapter 27

The morning the footman found Vespucci on the floor was the same morning that Abriana and Serpina arrived from Venice. She was in a sad mood, depressed over the fact that the Contessa had died so suddenly. They weren't real friends. What saddened her was the mere fact that one day she was full of life, the next, she was lying in a coffin. The whole incident made her promise herself that she would live to the fullest. Life was just too short. Not to mention the fact that while in Venice, Abriana was overcoming with a new emotion that left her befuddled. She had a frightful assault of anxiety, and nearly made a fool of herself. Little did she know was that she had a panic attack, but that was a diagnosis that that no one would yet have a name for at least for another century.

She asked one of the servants if Signor Vespucci had arrived from Rome and was informed that he had indeed. In fact, he had just had breakfast and taken a walk.

"Good. Have someone find him and tell him if he would join me for lunch," she said.

"Yes, your ladyship." The footman bowed. He had wanted to tell her ladyship his concerns but hesitated. Servants did not speak unless spoken to, and disclosing to la donna conjecture on his part violated this strict code of behavior.

"Oh," Abriana continued, "Tell the major-domo that we are expecting Miss Martina Colon to join us. Have him serve lunch in the loggia."

"Si, donna Abriana." The manservant left.

Abriana then went up to rest and change, with Serpina following her. Abriana told Serpina to bring out a promenade dress. She had enough time to make herself presentable. It would not do for her to be seen by her future husband in such a state.

Abriana and Giaochinno finally met for lunch. Serpina saw Giaochinno first and was so startled that she emitted a small

"Oh." Abriana looked up, surprised to see Giaochinno, his eyes dark from lack of sleep, his clothes put on hastily. She stood up to embrace him.

"Caro mio, what is the matter?" "The matter?" Vespucci asked, confused.

"You look terrible," Abriana moaned.

"Oh…" he said, "I'm just tired. Very tired."

"Well, sit down. Serpina, pour Signor some tea."

Giaochinno stared at Serpina, face unreadable.

"Maybe we should call a Doctor." Unfortunately, Tebaldi was out of town. "Maybe you're coming down with something," Abriana said as she felt his forehead.

"No, I'll be fine. Really. Seeing you, I feel better already." He smiled weakly.

"Well, you are never going back to Rome. I see that it doesn't agree with you," Abriana said with finality. At this point, Martina arrived.

"Goodness, Gio! What happened?" she asked alarmed.

"Nothing's the matter," Vespucci sat down, beginning to lose patience. "Like I told Abriana, I'm just tired." He took his cup and sipped, well aware that all three women were studying him.

"So, how was Venice?" he tried to sound casual.

"Oh, dear." Abriana began, "it was dreadful. The priest arrived late, the mass went on forever. It was so hot inside this small chapel that was not designed to hold that many people."

"And the floral arrangements! Too many releasing an overpowering stench!" Martina lamented.

The two ladies then began a litany of what went wrong, down to the last detail. Giaochinno pretended to be interested in their tale, but did not hear a word they said. He found himself occasionally giving Serpina a fleeting look, studying her face.

As lunch ended, the three decided to read their lines. Giaochinno asked Abriana if it would be all right for Serpina to read Tebaldi's lines since he wasn't there. Abriana thought it a splendid idea. The play, which Tebaldi had entitled "The Fall of Atrides," featured a young and noble Atrides. The shepherd boy has just rescued the Princess Luestra from death. They fall in love and pledge eternal devotion. He leaves her for a while to tend to his ailing mother but promises to return. Meanwhile, Thanatos (death) arrives. Beguiled by Luestra's beauty, he falls in love with her. Thanatos proposes, but she declines his offer, stating that she loves no one else but Atrides. Thanatos threatens Atrides with a gruesome death if she does not choose him. However, if she does, then the youth will be immortal since "death will never pass his eyes." Luestra asks for some time to decide and consults the oracle. The Goddess Venus hears her plea and takes pity but does nothing. When Atrides returns, he accuses her of being unfaithful, because of her suspicious actions. She denies it. Atrides leaves as she meets with Death again. She agrees to his proposal. As they kiss, Atrides catches them and pulls a sword to kill himself. He finds out he cannot die and Thanatos reveals who he really is. The couple leaves and Atrides moans his sad existence. He screams for help and Venus appears, with the cord of his life from the muses. He tells her he would rather die than live this miserable existence. She cuts the cord and he collapses. Luestra is returned to earth, freed from her contract to find her lover on the ground. She clutches him, she begs Thanatos to bring him back, but he explains that by forcing his death, Venus has inadvertently killed his soul, not just his physical life.

Luestra then tells Thanatos to take her away, leaving Venus. Atrides and Luestra of course would be played by Giaochinno and Abriana. Martina would be Venus and Thanatos would be played by the playwright himself.

They began to read their parts, going through their scenes quickly, only stopping when their fellow actors suggested a better way to read a line. When they got to the part where Luestra met Thanatos, Martina suggested they stand up which they did.

Abriana spoke her lines as the Princess Luestra.

Luestra:"You startled me."

Giaochinno as Atrides, in apologetic fashion replied: "I'm sorry."

Luestra: You did. I thought you were away.

Atrides: I have returned.

Luestra: My love…Why do you look so angry?

Atrides: Because you have been unfaithful!

Luestra: No!

Atrides: Then tell me; who has been here?

Luestra: No one's been here!

Atrides: I know that a stranger has been here! One that speaks of love?

Luestra: I have loved no one but you, my dearest.

Atrides: Then why act in strange manner recently?

Abriana: What do you mean?

Abriana looked at Giaochinno and with a frown said "How does he know? I mean, there's nothing in the lines before it that gives him a clue."

"I guess when you know someone well enough, it shows," Giaochinno replied, feeling tired. It took a lot from him to focus. He promised that he would try to better, if only to please the woman who he loved so much.

"Maybe he's just one of those men who's always jealous, always mistrusting," Martina said.

"Well, let's continue." Gio said, but Abriana had put her manuscript down.

"I think not, Gio dearest. You need to rest."

"As La Donna wishes." He acquiesced to her decision.

"I think Dottore Tebaldi likes me." Martina confessed. Abriana laughed.

"It's true! Why am I to play Venus, then?"

"Dottore Tebaldi is a married man." Gio stated, making an effort to be part of the conversation.

"Just because he's married doesn't mean he can't like me."

"Well then, shall we meet again tomorrow? Say for tea?" Abriana suggested. They all agreed. Martina left the couple.

"Gio, mio. Are you sure you are all right? I have never seen you in such a state."

Giaochinno was torn between telling her about Vincenzo. Finally, as a compromise, he said "Vincenzo was here yesterday."

"Why didn't you ask him to stay?"

"I didn't get a chance to. Anyway, he and I had an

argument."

"Is there ever a time that you two have a civil conversation?"

"I don't think that's possible anymore, cara mia. Vincenzo is full of hate, full of a poison that is eating him slowly but surely."

"I don't know what to say my love," Abriana said. She held Gio's hand and kissed it. "Tell me." "Ah, I cannot," Gio sighed.

"But why? Maybe we can help him," she suggested.

"Why would you want to help him?" Gio disengaged his hand from hers. "You don't even know him."

"I know you. He is your brother, your twin brother. That means that you and he are bound by the same goodness."

"No!" he cried. "He is the opposite of me. Goodness to him is what I find repulsive, and distasteful …and … and…" He tried to find the words but failed. "I cannot tell you anymore. I would be betraying him." He cried in anguish.

"My love," she held him, "I will do anything in my power to help him, to help you. But you must tell me all. Don't shut me out, Gio, please." She felt hot tears stream down her face. But Giaochinno remained silent, with only an occasional sound of despair escaping from him.

Serpina did not know what to do. The couple had obviously forgotten all about her in this tender and fragile moment. She slowly backed away and went back inside. She stood with her back pressed against the wall. She hated this Vincenzo. She hated him with all her might and all her soul, just as much as she loved Giaochinno Vespucci.

Chapter 28

That very night, as the winds once again rustled the leaves outside the window, Giachinno woke up drenched in sweat. "Vincenzo?" he cautiously and quietly called out.

There was no one, though. He walked toward the balcony. Pushing the billowing drapes away, he stepped out into the terrace. A figure, not too distant, walked on the grass, away from the house. Giaochinno had wanted to call out but was afraid of waking the sleepers in the house. He ran out of his room, grabbing a robe. He ran down the hall, down the stairs, past another corridor and finally through the room that led to the loggia. He flung open the doors and made his way to the garden. He stopped. A little bit farther, he saw a tiny light hover in the darkness. He ran for it.

When he finally caught up with the figure, he called out.

"Vincenzo!"

The figure turned. He realized it wasn't Vincenzo, but Serpina, who wore a cowled robe.

"Signor Vespucci!" she cried out in alarm.

"What are you doing out here?"

"Vincenzo. I thought you were him."

"So I was right."

"Right? Right about what, Serpina?" Gio asked, still panting from his recent exertion.

"I had spoken to the other servants," she said. "They have heard you speaking to someone in your room, not just last night but several times before that. How does he get up to your room without anyone seeing him? I wondered. I found out that you sleep with your balcony doors wide open. There is a large olive tree right next to that balcony." "Yes, yes..." Gio's breathing was beginning to normalize.

"A tree whose branches are large enough to support a grown man. Vincenzo is here, I just know it."

Gio marveled at the girl's deductive process.

"And what would you do if you found him?"

"I don't know. But I was going to plead with him to stop tormenting you."

"He doesn't really..."

"I've seen your pain," Serpina said bravely.

"You carry it secretly, but I see it with my heart."

"My dear Serpina," Gio murmured. Serpina felt a small thrill to be addressed so lovingly by such a man. "You must promise me that you will never, ever look for him."

"But he needs to be told!" she countered.

"No. There is no talking to him, Serpina."

"Why don't you just tell him to leave you alone?"

"I cannot!" Giachinno said, discouraged. "It's not that simple."

Serpina looked in the direction of the forest where the garden ended.

"I have failed him once," Giachinno continued. "I couldn't protect him. For the longest time he couldn't forgive me. But then he finally did. That was the happiest day of my life. I was complete again. It was me and him again. I wasn't lonely anymore. I had a brother again. I was complete."

"I assure *il Signor* that so many love him. He will never be lonely." That was as close as she could get to sharing her true feelings.

"I take it you have never had a brother, Serpina. There is a bond that cannot be broken. I cannot break that for which will kill me." Giaochinno said softly.

Serpina began to walk towards the forest again. Giaochinno took after her and grabbed her wrist. As he did this, she turned. The light of the lamp gave her an appearance of someone older and wiser. He stared at this face, stared at the scar on her forehead.

"I knew you would come to my rescue, our rescue. But you don't understand, mama," Gio said in a small voice. "He wants to kill you."

"Kill me. Why?"

"That's just it. I told him you didn't know."

"Know what?"

"What happened," Gio said with insistence.

"Signor Vespucci, what happened?" Serpina asked.

Gio looked shaken and confused all at the same time.

"Serpina?" he whispered. "Serpina!" he said once again, the sound of his own voice shocking him. "If you have any respect for me, you will stay away from the forest, from Vincenzo. If you see him, run away and hide. Please promise me."

Serpina lowered the lamp. "I promise, Signor," she said timidly.

They walked back towards the house, each quiet, lost in their own thoughts.

The next day, Abriana noticed that Giaochinno seemed better. He was dressed in a more elegant cut than the previous day's clothes. He stated that he was looking forward to all four of them having a 'run-through', reading (and acting) the play from beginning to end. He had even assigned Serpina the task of prompter, a person who would coax the actors if they forgot their lines. Doctor Tebaldi was a fine director, but also a comical one.

He had the ladies laughing several times and even Gio found himself chuckling here and there. They were to meet twice more.

Just then, a liveried male servant came in with a small silver tray in hand. He placed it on the table next to Giaochinno who opened and read it. He shook his head.

"What's wrong?" Abriana asked.

"It's a note. From Vincenzo. He is leaving for L'Aquila." L'Aquila was a hundred and fifty miles south, south east of Florence.

"What's in L'Aquila?" Abriana asked, confused.

With a dazed look and a hoarse voice, Gio answered, "Palazzo Gaspari."

Chapter 29

The Conte Emanuele Gaspari had always been in ill health. When he had met the twins, he already was overweight and suffered from a multitude of respiratory ailments. He always had the best care at the time, and given his passion for living, dismissed the aches and pains that plagued him and just ventured on. However, the last month saw him get progressively worse.

It began almost five or six weeks ago when Emanuele complained of a slight fever. Not a stranger to feeling ill, he merely dedicated himself to bed. But after a week, the fever had not gotten better, despite the home remedies of everyone in the Gaspari household. The local doctor was called. He prescribed the extract of willow bark as being the effective cure for Gaspari's malady. He reported good results from his patients. (Little did the doctor know at the time that willow bark extract did have a genuine ingredient - salicylic acid; today's aspirin.)

He felt a little better for a day or two, but then his fever began to worsen. This time, physicians from Milan, Rome and Pisa were summoned. By the time the physicians did arrive, they found the patient presenting a lattice-like rash on his chest and back. He also complained of joints, painfully swollen. The doctors were of the same prognosis. They shook their heads because they had seen too much of the same case. It was the same illness that had swept across Europe and had claimed thousands of lives, Mozart being one of them. This was Rheumatic fever. The doctors drew straws as to who would tell the Conte to put his affairs in order.

Although quite rare and highly treatable in the

present time, the diagnosis of rheumatic fever was a death warrant in the 1800's. There were no antibiotics to speak of, and some of the cures did not help at all. Still, Gaspari remained lucid and alert. He was also extremely irritated with anything and everyone. He had begun to suffer from repeated bouts of diarrhea and vomiting. Already heavy, he swelled so much more that his bed clothes would no longer fit him. New ones had to be made.

Aware that he had not much time on earth, he began to call on the few people that made him happy. One letter he dictated went to his younger brother, traveling abroad. He would now be the new Conte, heir to the land, the Palazzo, the Castile, everything that Emanuele possessed. The other letter was sent to Olivia Du Rhein, whom he had a momentary affair. She was a German lady of some royal ancestry who at one point Emanuele considered marrying. However, she left him shortly when she realized his true nature. She had caught Gaspari in bed twice, the first with a woman, the next with a man. Finally, the third letter he sent to Florence. He needed to know he was forgiven for what he had sanctioned fifteen years ago.

As the illness progressed, his heart was weakened.

The younger brother had sent correspondence ahead that he would hasten to L'Aquila. The lady came and visited briefly. She held Gaspari's hand and cried quietly. Gaspari looked at her. "Don't cry Olivia. I am not dead yet," Gaspari wheezed. A servant later recounted, (Although it remains a rumor and unfounded) that the Aryan mistress replied; "that's why I'm crying."

A few more people came and went to pay their

respects, many of them hoping that their superficial devotion would not be lost to the Conte, who may still bequeath them money, a painting, or some other token. He did not see but a few, the rest were sent away. He was beginning to suffer from delirium, the next to the last stage of the disease. The final one would be a coma.

Giaochinno arrived shortly after the people were sent home. When he saw the rooftop of the Palazzo Gaspari, he broke out into a cold sweat. He wondered if Vincenzo had gotten there before him.

Giaochinno was immediately ushered into his old patron's bedroom. When he entered, a few monks were kneeling at the foot of the bed, praying. He sat by the Count's huge bed and kissed him on the cheek. He had forgiven him.

"Giaochinno," Gaspari said weakly.

"Si, Signor Conte." Gio answered sweetly.

"Ah…I've always loved you most. You are like the son I never had." He placed his swollen hand on Vespucci's head. It did not stay there long. It flopped back down.

"I will always be grateful for your patronage."

"And how is your father?"

"He is…dead, your lordship," Giaochinno answered.

"No….he isn't dead. I saw him yesterday. I gave him money."

"Oh, my lord." Giaochinno touched Gaspari's cheek lightly."

"Remember when Vincenzo's voice cracked. I was so upset. I told him about it."

"You told him? When, Signor Conte?"

"A few minutes ago. He was sitting right there,

where you were sitting." Emanuele tried to raise his head but could not.

"He hasn't forgiven me." Gaspari continued softly. "He hasn't forgiven me."

From the corner of the darkened room came the familiar voice of Vincenzo. "And why should I forgive you, you bastard."

"Vincenzo!" Gio cried.

"He deserves to die a worse death than this!" Vincenzo announced.

"Will you please keep quiet? Can you not give him the silence he deserves?" Gio said through clenched teeth. The monks stopped praying.

"Vincenzo," Gaspari called out, "I didn't mean for it to happen like that. I didn't."

"He says he forgives you, my lord," Gio said.

"I do not. Don't you send him to the afterlife with that lie!" Vincenzo approached Gaspari but Giaochinno blocked him.

"This was a man who only knew beauty. All his life," Giaochinno defended his patron. Vincenzo finally backed away.

"Beauty? This man was evil, and he deserves to go to hell!" Vincenzo stormed out of the room.

"I'm sorry. He is obsessed with grief. He didn't mean to say what he said." Giaochinno apologized to the monks. The monks looked at each other. Finally one monk began his chanting, and was followed by the others. Giaochinno left the room to look for his brother.

Chapter 30

Abriana had taken a nap, which gave Serpina a brief respite for at least half an hour. After making sure that La Donna Abriana was resting comfortably, she left to have a word with the cook regarding her mistress' latest instructions. Walking along the corridor, she passed Vespucci's room. She stopped for a moment. She looked behind her and around, making sure there was no one. She opened the door and quickly entered. She didn't know what she was looking for. Perhaps it was mere curiosity on her part. Perhaps she was looking for a clue. Whatever the case was, she began to go through the room. There was nothing remarkable in the Gentleman's wardrobe, or the highboy for that matter. She then went to the desk and pulled open the larger, middle drawer. It was empty except for a few papers and an envelope. She took the envelope and opened it. It contained only one article, a photograph hidden beneath the folds of a beautifully embroidered handkerchief. She looked at it and was suddenly hit with a sudden realization. The photograph was a familiar face to her. She turned the picture over and read the message written in an awkward hand. It read: "To my beautiful Gio and Vincenzo - your mother."

She put the photograph back in the envelope and returned it to its original place. She took one more look before she left the room. As she made her way down the hall, her mind kept returning to the woman in the picture. She couldn't shake her astonishment.

At the Palazzo Gaspari, Gio was escorted by one of the older male servants to his room, where he found his brother sitting on the edge of his bed. The footman assigned to him proceeded to unpack his things but Giaochinno sent him away, politely asking him to come back later. He didn't want the servant to be the next victim of Vincenzo's ire.

"Vincenzo," Giaochinno began.

"You did it to me again, you bastard." Vincenzo cut him off. "Why did you tell him that? I don't forgive him. I don't forgive him at all."

"Vincenzo," Giaochinno pleaded, "he is dying."

"Well, he isn't dead yet, is he?"

Giaochinno did not know what else to say. He had seen his brother like this in Florence. He knew that whatever he said next would result in an angry outburst. He decided to keep quiet.

"Well, what?" Vincenzo asked, waiting for Giaochinno to say something. Giaochinno said nothing, but began to unbutton his waist coat.

"Ah…so now you're not going to talk to me?" Vincenzo teased.

Giaochinno took off his coat and placed it on the bed.

"I know you and that little maid of yours went out looking for me."

"What are you talking about?" Gio was suddenly fearful. Not for himself, but for Serpina.

"What are you talking about?" he mimicked Gio, "Really, you're so stupid, Gio."

Giaochinno hated it when his brother mimicked him. To tell him to stop though was tantamount to admitting that it did bother him, and Vincenzo would do it again and again.

"You know, I like Abriana. She and I had a talk about

you," Vincenzo said.

"You lie." Giaochinno would not believe it.

"No, really, Gio. She asked me to stop arguing with you." Vincenzo studied his fingernails. "She also thought you were boring. She said she needed a real man."

"No," Gio said, as if the word itself had some power.

"She said you were probably a homosexual. Most eunuchs are, you know."

"Stop it." Gio replied with clenched jaw.

"She said that maybe I could teach you to be more manly," Vincenzo laughed.

"Stop it, I said."

"You know," Vincenzo continued, "she even flirted with me when you were in Rome."

"Ha! She wasn't even in Florence!" Gio said triumphantly.

"Of course not, stupid. I was in the Contessa Ricci's funeral too, you know."

"Contessa Ricci's funeral?" Gio's heart sank.

"Of course. I was in Venice the day before she arrived. Why do you think I wasn't in Rome with you?"

Giaochinno sat down. Why did Abriana not tell him? Or was Vincenzo really in Venice?

"Maybe you should kill her too. She's such a tramp," Vincenzo hissed.

They argued again, the argument the same as before. Giaochinno, feeling drained, let Vincenzo rant. He fell asleep on a chair, listening to Vincenzo's sermon.

Despite the physicians who announced that it would happen soon, possibly in a day or two, the Conte did not die, nor fall into a coma. He did call out weakly for his brother, for his mistress, for Gio and Vincenzo. He also called out for his mother who had been dead many years now. Three days went by. More visitors showed up, more monks and priests came to pray for his soul.

Giaochinno felt that he should go. Leave for Florence where Abriana was waiting for him. But that would not be proper. He had to be there till the end. It was the wish of a dying man. Meanwhile, Vincenzo's anger had cooled to a tolerable level. He still constantly taunted Giaochinno, calling him names, telling him how worthless he was. Gio quietly implored his brother repeatedly to cease from doing so. It seemed that Vincenzo was actually goading Giaochinno into hitting him. Gio, even though tempted, had to use every resource he had to stop himself from doing so.

On the night of the third day, Gaspari could barely move. His appearance was grotesque. Only one monk was left in the room, but he had gone to take a nap. He had, after all, kept vigil and stayed up for two straight days. Surely the old man wouldn't kick the bucket just yet. He had seen many people die, and Gaspari's respiration, though labored, was current and steady.

Gaspari woke up. Someone was calling his name. At first, he thought it was Fra Domenico, come to punish him for staying in bed all this time.

But the figure came closer.

"Ah..." he said hoarsely, "my dear boy."

"Why don't you just die, you bastard."

"So..." Gaspari gasped, "you haven't... really... forgiven me."

"No. In fact, just to prove it, I'm sending you to hell."

Gaspari's eyes widened in disbelief. Too weak to shout for help, Gaspari could only plead for a few more minutes to live.

"Forgive..." he wheezed. "Forgive..."

Strong hands pushed the pillow over his face. Gaspari still made a great effort to resist, struggling like a fish out of water. The man was on top of him, as he pressed the pillow down harder and harder, as if they were engaged in a sexual act.

Eventually, Gaspari ceased to move. The man removed the pillow. With mouth close to the dead man's ear, he whispered "I did this for me and my brother. May God have no mercy on your soul."

Chapter 31

Giachinno traveled back to Florence with a heavy heart. Vincenzo badgered Giaochinno constantly. In the carriage, Vincenzo continued to annoy him. He only stopped when they were a few miles from Florence.

When he got out of the carriage, Giaochinno asked Vincenzo to come down, but he refused, saying that he wouldn't set foot in a place where he wasn't wanted. Gio, knowing better than to beg, kept silent. Vincenzo said that he would be back, to expect him for dinner. He yelled "dinner" and waved as the carriage sped off.

When he entered the large foyer, a liveried footman met him, stating that La Donna Abriana and her party were waiting for him, assembled in the loggia. He nodded and followed the footman.

"Gio!" Abriana embraced him. She noticed he had lost some weight.

"Abriana, dearest!" he embraced her back.

"Ciao, Gio!" Martina yelled and waved from where she was sitting. Dottore Tebaldi came to embrace him too.

"You are just in time. We actually expected you a few days earlier."

"There were some complications," Gio said, palm open and upward to gesture that it was nothing.

"We are so sorry to hear of the Conte's passing away." Tebaldi offered his sympathies.

"He lived a full life," Gio stated.

A silence engulfed the company. Finally, Abriana said something.

"Serpina has been reading your lines remarkably well."

"Signor," Serpina did her small curtsy again. Gio did not notice how Serpina scrutinized him.

"Oh! Guess what?" he told Abriana almost eagerly, "Vincenzo is coming to dinner."

"My word!" Abriana exclaimed, surprised. "Serpina, run and tell the cook to create something special for dinner, tell him that aside from Martina and dottore, we are having a most special guest."

"Si, Donna Abriana." Serpina nodded and exited, taking small but quick steps.

"Oh, my. It will be wonderful! Is your brother married, Gio?" Martina asked excitedly.

"No, no he's not," Gio said.

"This is sounding better already," Martina remarked.

"I'm sure the other Signor Vespucci is equally talented and compassionate as his brother," Enrico Tebaldi said. "It will be a glorious event."

"Well, he is talented. He can also be difficult at times. Really." Gio apologized, trying to give them advanced warning.

"Well, I'll be the judge of just how difficult he can be." Abriana smiled at him. He looked at her quizzically for a moment. He smiled back, uneasily.

They went back to their rehearsal. Abriana, who had a good memory, still had a few problems with a couple of scenes. She promised Tebaldi though that she would work doubly hard. They talked about costumes and the sets they were having built. Chatting gaily, the foursome seemed happy. Happier still was Gio, who expected Vincenzo to arrive anytime soon. Perhaps he could stay at Palazzo di Tursi, and that they would be one happy family.

Chapter 32

The magnificent family dining room was resplendent that evening. The best china was laid out and the silverware gleamed. The servants, standing at attention, were wearing their finest costumes. The major-domo brought several bottles of wine from the wine cellar, some of them costing a month's wages.

Only the ticking sound of the large mantle clock invaded the thick silence that blanketed the room.

"Perhaps something very, very important came up." Abriana tried to sound gay.

"But of course. You know, I've missed so many important functions because I had to attend to pressing matters," Doctor Tebaldi added.

"God knows how many dinners I've been invited to, Gio, that I couldn't show up for." Martina, not to be left out, supplemented. All three were trying their best to minimize the non-appearance of Vincenzo Vespucci. Before dinner began, Gio was animated and merry. As the hour progressed with no Vincenzo in sight, he grew despondent. Finally, their bellies growling, Abriana suggested that they eat ahead. Vincenzo would turn up soon.

They all sat down, Giaochinno visibly upset, as the other three diners silently cursed Vincenzo for his absence. The servants came out with the food and began to serve. The cook managed to produce an exceptional menu, having been told of the dinner party only that morning. Not one of the servants would tell him that the guest of honor did not show up. He had spent the better half of the day tearing his hair out and spitting invectives as he created this culinary affair.

"The cook really outdid himself," Abriana tried to sound upbeat, but her declaration was as hollow as a spent kettle.

Gio murmured assent. He appreciated the sympathy that these three showed him.

"So, Abriana, I heard from Martina that you nearly fainted in Venice?" Tebaldi asked Abriana. Aside from his eagerness to start a new subject, he was also concerned over his friend's health.

"Oh, it was indeed frightful. It was hot and stifling. People crushing you all over."

"I never realized the Contessa was so popular," Martina said. She had also attended, although she did not travel with Abriana. "There were people there I haven't seen for ages."

Giaochinno remembered what Vincenzo had disclosed to him in Rome.

"Vincenzo was in Venice, too. He said he saw you there." Gio said.

"Perhaps he did," Abriana put down her fork and patted her lips with her napkin.

"No," he pressed on, "he said he spoke to you."

"That's possible," Abriana sighed, tired of the subject.

"What do you mean that's possible? Did you or did you not speak with him." Giaochinno felt the anger rising in him.

"Gio mio, I spoke to so many people that day, some I've met only once, briefly."

"You would have remembered Vincenzo."

"Gio, I was deathly ill. I practically ran out to get to the carriage. A man came up and started speaking to me. I don't know. I was close to fainting. Poor Serpina had to virtually carry me," Abriana explained.

Serpina! But of course, Giaochinno thought. Serpina was there too. She could tell him what Abriana and Vincenzo spoke about.

"So what happened then?" Gio asked.

"I don't remember much." Abriana took a drink from her glass.

"Maybe Serpina does," Gio said. "Will you call her for me, please?"

"Gio, so what if Vincenzo spoke to Abriana?" Martina interjected, taking her ladyship's side.

"Just have her called," he insisted.

Abriana pointed at one of the servers, waving her finger to call him. "Call Serpina, please." The servant left immediately.

"What did he say?" Gio wanted to know.

"I cannot recall, Gio. It was raining by the time we got out of that stifling chapel. Raining very hard. I stood under the awning being crushed on every side, watching the water come down." "Go on..." Gio prodded.

"I waited for the carriage to come up. Meanwhile, this feeling of dread, like I couldn't breathe, overcame me. As soon as the carriage was in sight, I dashed for it, with Serpina running after me."

At the mention of her name, the young girl came out of the kitchen door.

"Ah, Serpina, come here please."

"Si, Signor Vespucci?"

"Perhaps you can clear up something for us," Gio asked her gently. "Do you remember when you were in Venice with your mistress? Tell us, what happened after the funeral?"

"La Donna Abriana and I were there. We attended the funeral. I noticed la donna had turned ashen, she began to fan herself since it was frightfully humid."

"Go on to when you left."

"Si, Signor," Serpina said. "We had begun to exit. People were being impatient. They had heard the thunder and the rain starting to pelt the roof. La Donna pulled me, rushing to get out. We got to the gallery, where there was a canopy. The rain by now was coming down in torrents. People who were inside were trying to push those of us in the gallery. Because of the rain, the people under the canopy would not move, not till their carriage came up. All of a sudden, la donna ran. She ran towards our carriage, despite the downpour. I ran after her." "And the man?" Gio asked.

"The man?" Serpina was confused.

"Yes, the man who spoke to your mistress. Before she got on the carriage!" Giaochinno practically hissed the last word.

"Oh," Serpina remembered. "The man came from behind us. He pulled the step and opened the door for us. He was talking about something."

"And what did he say."

"My apologies Signor Vespucci," Serpina replied dejectedly, "but he wasn't addressing me, so I was not paying attention."

"You didn't hear a word, nothing at all?"

"No, Signor. Between the wind, the rain, my trying to get la donna inside…no., sir. I'm sorry." Serpina furtively looked at Abriana. A look not lost to Giaochinno, who found the whole tale strange.

"He was saying something about how sorry he was," Abriana added. "Sorry that he wasn't there on time. I kept saying that's alright. I don't know why I said that."

"So maybe Vincenzo did speak, or tried to speak to her," Martina said. "Really Gio, is it really so important?"

"Does this have anything to do with why he's not here tonight?" Doctor Tebaldi intervened.

"No, you're right, Martina. It's not important." Gio sighed heavily. "Thank you, Serpina. You may leave." Serpina murmured a welcome and left the way she entered.

They went back to eating, their conversation stilted. The whole evening spoiled.

Chapter 33

Doctor Tebaldi and Martina said their goodbyes and thanked Abriana for a wonderful dinner. They tried to make plans to meet again in the morning, before the Countess's birthday party, but found their schedules too demanding. Abriana assured Tebaldi that she would know all her lines by tomorrow. Giaochinno tried to be gentler, knowing that it was because of him that the evening was ruined. When the two had gone, Abriana had begged Giaochinno's leave. She said she was exhausted, felt ill and had a headache. She was actually still upset over how he questioned her.

He felt that he needed to apologize to her, to say something. However his anger, like an extinguished flame, still smoldered. All he could do was utter a terse goodnight. She took a deep breathe, exhaled, turned and walked away. Giaochinno felt miserable.

Serpina was tidying the room when her ladyship came in.

"Ah, Serpina. A wonderful dinner ruined!" She sat on the settee.

"I hope her ladyship was satisfied with my answers." Serpina offered.

"Oh, absolutely."

Abriana stood up again and walked to the little dresser. She picked up a bound manuscript and glanced at the clock.

"Serpina..." she said still looking at the clock. "I am going out for a little air. I am feeling very suffocated again. I should be back soon. You need not come."

"Yes, ma'am." she answered Abriana, who left taking

the manuscript with her.

Giachinno, downhearted, didn't immediately go to his bedroom. Low and disappointed, he wandered the halls of the Palazzo aimlessly. He studied the paintings on the wall, but found that his mind wandered instead to the conversation they had at dinner. Why couldn't Abriana say that she met with Vincenzo? Did she really not recall it? And why did Serpina look at Abriana like that? Could it be that Vincenzo was telling the truth? Could it be that Abriana did meet with him? He gripped his chest. Could it be that Vincenzo and Abriana were really seeing each other, behind his back? Annoyed by these thoughts, he gave up on looking at the works of art and decided the night air would do him well. He proceeded to find a way outdoors, to the gardens.

In the west garden, in a patch of grass closest to the side of the Palazzo, was an old but well maintained gazebo. The gazebo was actually made of reclaimed materials from a greenhouse built several years ago, when Abriana was still a child. However, a storm had long since demolished the greenhouse, leaving only broken glass, timber, and a copper covered cupola that topped its glass covered roof. Her grandfather, a frugal man who disliked throwing anything away, decided to build the gazebo with the leftover material. It was a simple but elegant structure painted white, with the same copper covered cupola sitting proudly on top of its wood shingled roof.

Abriana had always loved this gazebo. She used to play there as a child. Now, as an adult, she still visited occasionally. Tonight was one such occasion. She sat down and took a deep breath of the night air, suffused with the fragrance of the flowers in the garden. She placed the lamp, which she had carried from inside, on the top of the balustrade. In the dim light, in the quiet, she felt more relaxed. She opened the manuscript and began to read. She closed her eyes for a moment.

Giaochinno saw her. At first, he saw only the light. The light hovered, much like a firefly would. As the light grew closer, he realized it was Abriana, holding a lamp. He found himself inching closer behind the bushes, just a few feet from the gazebo. What was she doing here? She said goodnight. She said she was going to bed. She had a headache.

A light breeze blew. The leaves stirred. As the leaves rustled, a figure emerged opposite from where Giaochinno was hidden. His eyes widened as he saw his brother appeared. Abriana stood up. Vincenzo approached the gazebo and stopped right where the steps began. He whispered, 'Abriana.'

As Vincenzo stepped up the gazebo, she put the book down.

"You startled me," Abriana said.

"Did I now?" Vincenzo put his hands behind his back and walked a circle around her.

"You did. I thought you were away." She fanned herself with the pages.

"Abriana, I never really left. You should know that."

"My love", she hesitated a bit, "my love…Why do you look so angry?"

"Because you've been cheating on me," Vincenzo accused her.

"No!" she put her hand on her bosom, then again said "No," as she bit the back of her hand.

"No." she said again as she closed her eyes.

"I saw you with Giaochinno," Vincenzo said slowly, menacingly.

"No... one's... been... here!" She said empathically. She sat down and looked at the hem of her skirt.

"So now you'll tell me you love him?

"I have loved no one but you, my dearest," she whispered.

"Then you must choose. Choose! Giaochinno or I?" There was a short silence.

"Ah!!! Why does it have to be so difficult?" she cried, waving the book in the air.

"Everything is difficult." Vincenzo grinned at her. She yelled again, hastily stepping off the gazebo and running off towards the house, followed immediately by Vincenzo.

Giaochinno could not breathe. He stood in the shadows for a moment, trying to imagine that he was a fixture, not a man. Perhaps a lamp or a tree, one that did not feel.

Chapter 34

The next day, the entire Palazzo was in chaos. It was La Donna Claudia's birthday, and everyone was busy. Even though this party would not be as large as the masked ball, (only the friends closest to the family would attend.) What it lacked in quantity was made up in quality. Not to mention the fact that for the ball, outside help was hired. Tonight's festivities would utilize only the present staff.

Giaochinno went to Abriana's room but was told that she would meet with him at lunch. Lunch came but again was told that she had to fit the costume (for the play) and would not be available either. Giaochinno gave up. She was avoiding him, he thought. He ate lunch alone in his room. Tea came and went. His valet ran in and virtually dropped the service. He had other things to do today and tea was merely an inconvenience. Giaochinno waited to be summoned by her ladyship, but no one ever came. Finally, he dressed for the play. His costume was far simpler than that of the ladies. It was a toga. He donned the hose and sat down. Vincenzo and Abriana! He could not get that scene out of his mind.

The guests had settled down. The Marchese came up, positioned himself in front of the heavy curtain that separated the audience from the small stage. He welcomed all of them. He stated that for La Donna Claudia's gift, her daughter had put enormous time and effort into her mother's gift. She would offer a play. A Greek tragedy. La Donna Claudia laughed and clapped her hands. The others followed suit. The Marchese thanked them again, and hoped they enjoyed the play and left the stage.

Meanwhile, behind the curtains, Gio was desperately trying to have a word with Abriana. Abriana was beautiful in her pale green, Grecian robe, hair made up. A seamstress was still hemming the long skirt.

"Oh, Gio, you do look so handsome!" she said when she saw him.

He gazed at her. She was so beautiful. His heart ached.

"Poor major-domo. He's sweating like a pig. He's such a darling to do it though." She giggled.

"Abriana," he started.

"And you should see Doctor Tebaldi. So fearsome!" she put on a face of mock viciousness.

There were just too many people around, too many things happening. He couldn't get a word in. Then he heard the Marchese talking.

"Places!" hissed Doctor Tebaldi.

Abriana turned around but Giaochinno grabbed her by the wrist. "Where were you last night?" he asked.

"Gio, I need to be on stage!" she replied.

"Where were you last night?" he asked again.

"Where do you think I was last night?" she answered in frustration.

"You said you had a headache."

"And I did."

"You said you were going to bed," he said strongly.

"And I did, Gio, I didn't go anywhere last night."

She was lying to him, he knew it. He let go of her.

When the curtains were parted, Abriana shrieked, alarming many in the audience. Their shock slowly faded however, when they realized it was only a part of the play. Abriana, on stage, was trying valiantly to escape the clutches of a creature that could be best described as a Minotaur. The 'Minotaur' was actually the major-domo who had been coerced to put on the heavy, papier-mâché bull head and heavier, wooly costume. The people began to applaud and cheer, to acknowledge they've been fooled by Abriana. Abriana began her short monologue.

Giaochinno then came out, and was cheered again. Many of the women craned their necks to see such a handsome youth so scantily clad. With sword in hand he chased the creature offstage. A piercing growl was heard, and Giaochinno entered again, with the head of the monster in one hand and his bloodied sword in the other. The spectators applauded again. Martina came out in a dazzling costume of beaded silver sequins and a large equally stunning head dress. There was more applause, although one couldn't be sure if it was for Martina or the outfit.

As the couple gazed at each other, Martina, who played the goddess Venus, began to tell of what had just transpired. Abriana and Venus left Giaochinno to list his qualities. He claimed to be strong, brave, noble and admirable. The audience believed him.

The play went on without any problems, until one scene. Giaochinno entered the stage and sees Abriana, sitting on a realistic looking boulder, caressing her face. Abriana began her lines as the Princess Luestra: "You startled me."

Giaochinno as Atrides, replied in a sarcastic tone replied: "You were expecting my brother?" None in the audience gave an inkling that they didn't understand.

Abriana was thrown off, not knowing what to say. She looked at Serpina who could only mouth the words 'I don't know'.

She immediately took control. "I was startled because I thought you were away."

"I have returned." Giachinno answered. He realized that his anger made him speak something else.

"My love…Why do you look so angry?

"Because you have been unfaithful." Giaochinno replied without acting angry. In fact, he sounded lost, resigned. The play went on.

After the play, the four characters came out to bow and was highly applauded. After a few curtain calls, the curtains fell back. Abriana, Tebaldi and Martina were all busy congratulating each other, filled with vivacity that performers feel after performing. Giaochinno tried his best not to seem ungentlemanly. The Marchese and Claudia went backstage to commend them, and told them to hurry and change. Dinner would be served soon. Gio cursed under his breath that he wouldn't have a chance to speak with Abriana.

They all changed and joined the group that was already having dinner. Unfortunately, Abriana was seated far away from Giaochinno, who had to bear being civil to a boring woman to his left who went on and on about his performance.

At the end of the dinner, the men retired to the library were they would drink their brandy and smoke their cigars. The Marchese pulled Giaochinno just as he was about to approach Abriana. The wealthy man wanted his future son in law to join them. The women meanwhile, stayed to gossip.

Giaochinno drank more brandy than he should have.

Chapter 35

The male guests were still having a heated discussion on politics. An hour and a half had gone by. Giaochinno, bored by the conversation, decided to swipe another bottle of brandy and leave. He went over to one of the servants, whispered something and stuffed a bill into his pocket. The servant came back after a little while, not with a bottle of brandy, but a bottle of dessert wine instead. Gio didn't care. He saluted the man and slowly made his way to the nearest exit. Luckily, the servant had enough foresight to have already uncorked the bottle.

He went outside. The moon was full, he noticed. He uncorked the bottle and took a large swallow. The wine was sweet, unlike the brandy that burned his throat. He walked and made it to the gazebo. How could they do this to him? The two people he loved had betrayed him! He began to sob.

When the guests had all gone home, Abriana began to wonder where Giaochinno went. No one had seen him. She had Serpina go knock on his door. While she waited for her maid to return, she saw one of the male servants walk past her. She asked him if he had seen the gentleman. He replied that he last saw Signor Vespucci enter the lesser ballroom where they just had the play. She went immediately.

She entered the semi-darkened room. The curtains were once again parted, and sitting on the floor, beside the faux boulder were two or three empty bottles.

"Gio?" she called softly. Giaochinno came out from behind the curtains.

"What?" he growled.

"Gio. You startled me!" she said, trembling.

"I'm sorry." Giaochinno mockingly replied.

"I looked all over for you. I thought you left the Palazzo." She approached him.

"I have returned," Gio said dramatically.

"Gio, my love," she said, "Why are you so angry?"

"Because you have been unfaithful! Both of you!"

"Giaochinno, what are you talking about."

"Tell me, Abriana, is he still here?"

"Who?"

"I know that Vincenzo was here. He was here last night." Lightning crashed outside, revealing Giaochinno's face. It was a face she had never seen before and she was truly scared.

"Gio, you're drunk! You're not making sense."

"I saw you last night! I saw you by the gazebo. I was hidden." Gio slowly approached her.

"You were there?"

"Yes. I saw you!" The wind blew outside, as a shutter banged, making Abriana jump. Suddenly, Gio heard laughter from the stage. Gio spun around. From behind the curtain, Vincenzo appeared, laughing.

"I guess the game's up Abriana. He saw us."

"What did you see?" Abriana peered into his eyes.

"What do you think I saw? Oh…" he moaned, "I have loved no one but you, my dearest." He mimicked her.

"I was acting!" she said, her voice nervous.

"Yes, Gio." Vincenzo laughed menacingly. "We were both acting!"

"Why? Why?" Gio asked.

"Because I needed to rehearse," she stammered.

"Yes, Giaochinno." Vincenzo said, his words dripping

with insincerity.

"I don't believe you! I don't believe you." Gio put his hands on his hair as if to tear it.

"Come on Abriana. Stop tormenting the fool. Just tell him the truth. You think he's a faggot."

"I am not a faggot!" Gio shrieked.

"Gio," Abriana was beginning to panic. "Please Gio, let's go upstairs."

"I wouldn't go anywhere with you, you tramp. You whore! You traitor!"

"Gio, there's no one but you," Abriana said frightened.

"It's true. I made love to her, but that doesn't mean anything."

"You made love to him? You…made love…to him?" he was screaming at her.

"Gio, that's a lie! I haven't made love to anyone."

Giaochinno pulled out a knife. His father's knife.

"Gio, what are you doing. No!" Abriana tried to escape but Gio lunged at her and caught her. His father's knife plunged it into her chest once, twice, three times. She fell to the floor. Another scream.

Serpina had entered the room.

"You knew! You knew! You could have prevented this." Gio pointed the knife at her.

"Signor Vespucci!" Serpina cried. Gio dropped to his knees and clutched Abriana's lifeless body.

Vincenzo came close.

"I'm sorry Gio." Vincenzo said with a slight cheeriness to his voice.

"I'm going to kill you too."

"Well, don't take all day, you faggot." "Gio!" Serpina

finally said his name.

"Help me." He looked at Serpina.

"Help me, Mama, please." He cried. "You didn't help the first time. Now's your chance…"

Serpina took the knife away. A French door leading outside banged open, letting in the wind and the rain. Giaochinno looked and saw Vincenzo wave goodbye.

"Oh, Gio…" Serpina was crying.

Chapter 36

The Palazzo di Tursi was boarded up. The Marchese and his wife didn't want to set foot in it again. They gave all the servants an adequate sum, each as severance (which wasn't required of them) and wrote letters of reference. The artwork was sold at auction, and so were all the furnishings. The Marchese then announced to everyone that he and his wife were moving, possibly to Milan, where his brother and two sisters still lived. Florence had become unbearable for them.

They also bequeathed Serpina a goodly amount, to be drawn every month, held in trust for her. She would live in relative comfort for the rest of her life.

Serpina worked as Martina's maid for a while, but eventually left her employment in good terms. She also met a man. The man was a few years her senior. He was kind and scholarly, not very rich but neither was he poor. When he proposed, she said yes. She liked him immensely but didn't love him. Still, he was an admirable man and she grew to love him. She never told him what happened at Palazzo di Tursi.

Before she left the Palazzo, she went back to Vespucci's room. She took the photograph in the envelope. For several years she kept it. After a year, she gave birth to a son. She named him Giaochinno.

Chapter 37

Bennett could scarcely believe the tale that he just heard. Vespucci once again sat on the corner, on his haunches, humming to himself.

"Signor Vespucci?" he called to the man twice, but there would be no response. Just like a star on nova, Giaochinno Vespucci had shown dazzlingly, only to burn up too fast.

Bennett looked out, only seeing clouds reflecting a golden reddish sky. The door opened and Dottore Uberto peered inside.

"Are you finished?" Uberto asked.

"I think we are." Bennett replied. He followed Uberto out but stopped and turned. *"Grazie, Signor Vespucci, grazie mille,"* he said respectfully.

Uberto closed and locked the door behind him.

"Come," he said to Randolph. "Let us see what you found out."

They walked. The stench of the corridor assailed his nostrils again. The hall was emptier now, less busy.

"So, do you feel you made progress?" Dottore Uberto asked.

"Yes, yes I think I did."

"And the key? What was the key he was talking about?"

"Oh! That. It was B-minor."

"The key of…B?"

"Minor."

Dottore Uberto laughed. "I should have known. He kept talking about the key. I thought he wanted a key to get out, now I realize it was a key to get in. To get into his mind."

"Yes. Apparently, he felt that he could only afford to tell this tale to one who shared his passion." "So, what are your preliminary findings?"

"The patient had a very traumatic childhood, beaten by his father, sold and finally castrated, together with his twin brother. Upon adulthood, the stress of fame, questions of his sexual identity, became a precursor to his murderous rampage. Of course, his brother was the one who drove him to it."

"What about his brother?" Dottore Uberto asked, as he opened the door to his office.

"My goodness! That one's the real crazy one." Randolph stated empathically.

Uberto told the secretary to bring coffee.

"I can assure you, he is not crazy." The older doctor grinned.

"Okay, here we have the older twin, Gio, who is good and noble. Then we have Vincenzo, the antithesis of his brother. Did they ever catch him?"

"Vincenzo?" Doctor Uberto asked.

"Yes."

"Randolph," Dottore Uberto put his hand on the young man's shoulder and looked deeply into his eyes with love and kindness. "Vincenzo died during the castration process. There is no Vincenzo. Never was."

A hundred scenes flickered before Bennett's eyes. Abriana and Serpina and Vincenzo and Gaspari and Lorenzo and...Giaochinno.

"Christ!" Bennett cried.

"I think you American's say 'God damn it', also."

The secretary came in with two steaming cups of

coffee.

"That can't be. Vincenzo was there. He was the one who…" Bennett stopped.

"When the carabinieri arrived, Giachinno was ranting and raving about many things. One of them was that Vincenzo and Abriana were lovers. The truth was eventually found out. Then there is the case of Serpina, the maid. She showed up in my office several years ago, right when they transferred him here. She said it was time for her to finally give Vespucci up for lost. She gave me a lot of insight. She also left me this." Uberto took a picture out of an envelope and placed it in front of Randolph. "This is a picture of Gabriella Vespucci."

"Yes?" Randolph took the picture.

"You could also say it is a picture of Serpina."

"I don't follow." Bennett looked at the photograph again.

"Serpina looked remarkably like Gio's mother. In fact, when Serpina visited, he kept calling her 'Mama'. He and his psychic twin who lived within him felt abandoned. One part of him cherished and loved her. The other hated her for not rescuing them, protecting them, preventing their castration." Uberto explained patiently.

"Freud would have a lovely time with that."

"A little like an Oedipal tragedy?" Uberto inquired.

"He mentioned that…a tragedy," Bennett said.

"Really?" Uberto said.

"He mentioned that they did a play. When he was talking about what made it tragic, he recounted something. Let me see…" Randolph glanced at his notes.

"He stated that a true tragedy must have 'a dynamic contest between two opposing forces.' Something about good versus good."

"This must have been that Greek play that Serpina had told me about." Uberto put his hand on his chin.

"Yes, precisely."

"You did make headway. Please share some more." Uberto encouraged him. Randolph recounted the whole story, from beginning to end. When he got to the part where Giachinno accused Abriana of meeting Vincenzo in Venice, Uberto stood up.

"Ah! Now it makes more sense." The older doctor exclaimed.

"What makes sense?"

"Serpina mentioned something about a stranger in Venice. She said she eventually remembered who it was later on."

"Who was the stranger?" Bennett wanted to know.

"She said it was the groom. The footman who helped passengers in and out of the carriage. She said before leaving the Palazzo he came up to her, to wish her good luck and apologized for his inattentiveness that one rainy afternoon in Venice. I didn't know why she made sure I knew that fact."

"I see." Bennett thought about it for a while. They drank their coffee in silence. Each man lost in thought.

"So, Randolph." Uberto lowered his cup. "If you were Gio, would you choose to accept your fate, or will you swear revenge?"

Bennett was quiet, trying to find the right answer.

"It is not so easy, is it?" Uberto smiled at him.

"To choose between good and good."

"But how can you say that killing someone is good?"

"How can you say that letting a murderer go free is

good?" Uberto countered.

"I see your point," Bennett agreed. "So the real illness here was not his delusion, but his inability to accept his brother's death, to accept his nature, to accept his future."

"No, Doctor Bennett. I think the real illness here is that when Vincenzo died, a part of his soul died with him. The part that died festered and decayed. It began to spread like a cancer, eating at him, and spewing out a reality that was easier to deal with. No, my dear Doctor Bennett. The real illness here was hoping against hopelessness."

Epilogue

Randolph met with Uberto in his office one last time. The secretary let him in and told him that Uberto would be back shortly. As he waited, he looked around. It was an average office, but spending time there with his mentor, it had become familiar, almost like a second home. The door opened. Once again, Randolph was welcomed with that recognizable, gap-toothed smile. They spent a few moments talking about nothing, each man trying desperately to find the right words to say that he would miss the other one. But like men, they could not. Instead, they spoke about plans.

Finally, Randolph stood and thanked the doctor for his guidance. He promised that he would write often. Dr. Uberto promised that he would reply, and may visit America if the opportunity presented it. Randolph presented his right hand, so that they could shake hands. Uberto instead smiled at him, let out a growl and grabbed him, embracing him tightly. Randolph laughed and hugged back.

The larger man kissed him on both cheeks.

"You will 'be good', no?" Uberto winked.

"Si, Dottore mio. I will be very good," he said.

He tried his best not to cry as he left the room.

Bennett made his way down, past the lobby, waving goodbye to the stoic matron sitting at her station. He pushed the doors of the main entrance and walked out. The doors banged open.

Dusk had lengthened the shadows on the street of the Via San Gallo, Randolph noticed. With the sun about to set, he saw the city bathed in a golden light. Randolph took a few steps and found himself on the sidewalk. A gas lamp lighter had just passed him, did not notice him in fact, for the old man was walking away hurriedly. He took a few more steps and looked up the imposing hospital. He thought he heard singing but it could have been the wind. He felt a breeze blow gently on his face. He heard the rustle of leaves sweeping past his feet.

Bennett could not decide whether to go back to the hostel or to just walk around. As he stood there uncertain of his next destination, he noticed another man across the street walking away from him. Bennett stared, squinting slightly. The man was right about to turn the corner when he stopped, turned and looked at Randolph. The man smiled at him, waved quickly and disappeared. Randolph shook his head, as if to clear it.

He took a few hurried steps towards the direction of where the man turned the corner before disappearing, but stopped. Bennett smiled and shook his head again. He slowly turned around and proceeded the opposite way, as if he forgot something. For a moment there, Randolph could swear the man he saw turn the corner looked like he was Vespucci's twin.

Printed in Dunstable, United Kingdom

71997203R00131